Scratches across the Surface

1946

Ladies of Bottlebrush Grove

Olwyn Harris

Stand firm in the faith;
be courageous;
be strong.
Do everything in love.
(1 Corinthians 16: 13,14)

Published by: Reading Stones Publishing
Helen Brown & Wendy Wood
Woodwendy1982.wixsite.com/readingstones
Cover Design: Olwyn Harris Some of the cover elements were created using
AI technology.

For more copies contact the publisher at:

Glenburnie
212 Glenburnie Road
ROB ROY NSW 2360
Mobile: 0422 577 663
Email: Readingstonespublishing@gmail.com

Dedication:

For my Mum, who showed me scratches don't steal beauty...
Faith was part of her courageous beauty.

I.

"Faith? Faith Galloway? You are back?"

She turned around and stared at the man behind her. "Oh. Well, if it isn't one of the infamous Trimboli cousins. It has been a while Gabe. How have you been?"

"Well, you know. The funeral was... a funeral. Did you go? I'm sorry... I didn't see you there. Lots of people."

"Ma'ma wrote to me, but I didn't get back in time. I only arrived in town yesterday. Your grandmother was like family to me. I am very sorry for your loss Gabe. She will be missed by many people." Faith sighed. Missed by me.

"Hey, do you have time for cup of coffee? A friendly face is doing me well."

She hesitated and nodded. "Sure..." They sat down at a café and ordered. "So how is your family doing?" Faith swallowed, and made herself take another mouthful. How did she think they would be? They had just buried a loved one. She knew what that was like.

"It doesn't matter that Nonni had a good innings; it only matters that she was family. I miss her so much."

"Of course..."

"Papa has taken it pretty hard. Christmas was pretty much cancelled, given the circumstances. Mamma was a rock about it. Decorated the tree and baked a cake. Keeping everyone on track, like she does."

"It seems to be the Italian way. Strong women who hold their families together. Your grandmother definitely had that way about her."

"Yeah. She did..."

"That, and a good pot of risotto always on hand. I remember those family dinners with affection."

"Nonni's risotto is the best..." Was.

"Your brothers and cousins... have they left now? After the funeral..."

"Ahh... most of them still live around here. Those who made it through the war came back. Unlike others, they still call Lenwick home." He said it good naturedly, but there was a twist to his mouth that made his point. "When do you go back to the city? I heard you were engaged."

She blushed. Noted the reproach and dropped her hand into her lap out of sight, tracing the ring on her finger. It was large and expensive. Embarrassingly extravagant in these times. "I... um... I am. Yes."

"And your fiancé?"

"You are still very nosey, Gabriele Trimboli. My fiancé is fine. His name is... is Worsley Jones. He is very accomplished. An accountant. He works in a bank."

"Jones? Your ambition is to be Mrs *Jones*? That is a come down, as far as names go."

"The name thing is still annoying you. Why can you not let that go?"

"You refused to marry me because of my name. That is a rejection that would break any man's heart."

"I was nine years old!"

He laughed and shook his head. "Well, it seems you got what you wanted. A respectable English name. Although Jones sounds more like a commoner to me. And a banker... really? I'm not sure I would advertise that since everyone is still reeling from a worldwide financial depression flanked by a couple of world wars!"

Faith winced. "Worsley was not responsible for any of that. You paint my heart as hard and unfeeling, insensible to the tragedies we have all gone through." It was not an uncommon condition, for those trying to recover. Hard and unfeeling numbed the pain.

He shrugged. "Oh, I'm familiar enough with your inflexible temperament, to be sure. I decided a long time ago it is easier to work with wood than with your unyielding heart, Faith Galloway. But perhaps that is also what makes you steadfast and loyal. I would never say you were unfeeling though. That does not fit."

She shook her head and smiled. "I'm guessing that is carpenter-speak which actually means we are old friends."

"The oldest of friends... to be sure. It is definitely good to see you again."

Faith's voice went quiet. "Gabe, I was wondering if I could ask you something..."

"Sure, you can ask. No, I am not married. And no... there is no one on the horizon."

She laughed. "Well, that was not actually the question. Nor is that very Italian of you. I understood it was a Trimboli responsibility to be married by the time you were twenty-one. And to have fifteen kids by the time you are thirty. Very doable if you have any number of twins."

"Well, the war got in the way. I have definitely let the side down terribly. I did give it a shot. But it didn't work out."

"Oh. I'm sorry. What happened?"

"Cousin Franco."

"Franco? She left you for Franco? Oh, the poor dear. She is going to regret that move."

He grinned. "I can comfortably say I am not regretting it. It is one of those things that worked out for the best."

"What I really wanted to ask... was not the details of your marital status... although an interesting aside of trivia, it..."

"Not trivial to me, by the way."

"No... of course. What I wanted... I wondered if you would consider it inappropriate if I asked to rent a room at Nonni's house. She used to have boarders all the time. Just while I am here. I know it is soon, since... you know... but there doesn't seem to be many options in town, and I definitely don't want to go to either pub."

He went still and looked at her. "You're not staying at the farm? Is everything okay?"

"Sure. Yes. Everything is fine. My visit is just a short one. I need to organise some things for the wedding... it will be a small, private affair. I insisted we hold it in Lenwick because I didn't want to add pressure on Ma'ma needing to travel for the ceremony. Having it here also gives me a valid excuse for a much-needed holiday. But I still have work to catch up on, so I need quiet. Of course home is overrun with our unruly mob... with a couple of extras thrown in as usual. All my students' submissions will end up with any variety of unmentionable smears on their papers if I try to mark them at our family dining room table."

"Oh. Well. I can't see that it would be a problem using Nonni's place. Can't guarantee quiet though."

"What do you mean?"

"Well, I officially work for Trimboli Brothers now: Papa and Uncle Marco. Construction and renovations. I am fixing up Nonni's house so we can sell it. We wanted to do a repaint even before the war, but Nonni would never allow it. I always felt bad the house was getting so shabby, but you know what they say – a cobbler's kid always runs barefoot. She said there were more important things to be spending money on. So I will be working on it during the day. But it will be quiet enough in the evenings."

"Oh. Well, it actually sounds perfect. I don't mind navigating renovations. I will out at the farm a lot, so it won't make much difference to me. I can do my marking in the evenings... will be quieter than the pub, I am sure. What happened to your job at Wagner's workshop? I guess it closed during the war."

"True it did. I finished up with Henrik when I enlisted. You know, they sent him to The Farm during the war, because of his name and his accent." The Farm was a euphemism for a nearby military compound set up to detain suspicious residents who might jeopardise national security. Germans, Asians... all immigrants had to prove their patriotism. Every Trimboli enlisted for that very reason. Gabe shook his head and drained his coffee. "He was a good man and didn't deserve being a prisoner-of-war in his own country. I'd already left when he was arrested. It was wrong, beginning to end, and I feel terrible there was no one to advocate for him. Not that it would have made any difference. It just felt weird being posted to fight Henrik's kin when he looked after me so well. I never said anything of course, but it never sat right. Anyway, when I came back, I found Henrick's shop had been torched, so my plans to reopen it were also burnt."

"You liked him, didn't you?"

"Old Henrik was Fritz through and through. I think part of the problem was that he refused to anglicize his name. Saxton changed his name from Sultzer... and now he is running for Mayor. Henrik just said that is the name his parents gave him, and he wouldn't dishonour them. He was pedantic to a tee and an absolute genius with wood. He did his best with me, but it is a well-known truth that you can lead an Italian to water and all he will do is kick back and have a swim. I'm sure I was a frustration to him, just as much as I found his finicky expectations oppressive."

"And now you are doing houses instead?"

"Yeah. Nonni's house is my project. The benefit of that is you can stay for free. Wouldn't be right to charge rent when it is a building site."

"Oh. A building site. Are you sure it is okay if I stay?"

"Do you mean is it safe? I'm not demolishing it. What I am doing is mostly cosmetic. Bit messy maybe. What did you think 'navigating renovations' would look like?"

"Not as reassuring as I was hoping... but okay, fair enough. However, I will be obliged to contribute something if I'm staying there."

"Well, okay... if you must. How about you share your food with me? That will save me from having to grub meals for myself. Never liked cooking so I'd be very happy to hand that job over."

"Sometimes I wonder if you really are Nonni's grandson. How could you grow up with all her amazing food and not like cooking it?"

"I liked eating it..." he said with a grin.

"Do you need to talk with your family... to check they are okay that I stay there?"

"No. Not necessary. Like I said: I have oversight."

"Alright then. I will get my bags this afternoon. Are you *sure* I will not be in your way?"

"Let's just trial it... and if it's not to your liking you can always set up a barricade on your Mamma's table to dodge smears while you grade papers... or go to either one of the pubs and not sleep at all."

* * *

2.

Faith looked around the living room and shook her head at the chaos. Her family lived in a wind tunnel. It was a geographical phenomenon created by two-legged willy-willies constantly running whirlwinds through the house. Her mother rushed in with a baby who was screaming frantically. "Oh Faith! Thank goodness! Can you go and find where Jimmy is? He is somewhere cooking up trouble with Joe, I am sure. Oh dear! Who has taken the... Violet! What did you do with the saucepan? I need the saucepan!" She turned around in search for the elusive pan.

Faith shook her head and left. This life her mother had chosen was exhausting, and Faith was never really sure how she kept it up. Her mother had all but made the decision not to foster any more babies, when Dr Mortimer gave her the prescription for his *Special Tonic*. Being the custodian of that recipe was a responsibility aligned with safeguarding a priceless masterpiece. It meant any reputable chemist could consistently make up the tonic without a prescription. The gift was even more significant since it was one of the very last things Dr Mortimer gave her mother before his heart attack.

"Jimmy! Joe?" Faith called out and followed her nose towards the shed. "Joe! Where are you?" She smelt smoke.

She heard a squeal and running feet that came rushing out to bowl her over. "Faith! You are home!"

"Joe! There you are! Ma'ma sent me to find you both. Where is Jimmy?" she asked suspiciously.

"Practicing his fire sticks. But he's no good at it... so he's cheating with the flint."

She rushed around the back of the shed. Jimmy sat in a pile of hay, feeding a wispy flame with straw. Faith grabbed a bucket, dunked in it the water trough, dousing child and fire in a gush of water. He spluttered to his feet, angrily objecting to the interruption of his very good experiment. "James Galloway – what were you thinking? You cannot light a fire in the middle of a haystack!"

"I can, 'cause I did! I was doing okay, until you messed it up. Why did you do that?"

"Because..." She shook her head bewildered. If he ever arrived at adulthood with all limbs intact, it would be a miracle. "Because... I came to give you and Joe a hug, you ragamuffins! Please don't burn down the shed."

"Nah. It'll be okay. I'm getting better at it now."

"Pass over the flint. Now." Jimmy scowled and reached into his deep pockets and handed over the offending tool. "Where did you get this?"

"From Dad's bench. But I'm trying a strike plate as well. You can use any old piece of metal for that. That'd be handy if I'm ever caught in the bush without matches."

"Innovative no less. Come on... want some afternoon tea? I was going to make some scones."

"Faith – you never come home anymore! We miss you." Joe scraped his scuffed boot.

"I miss you too Buddy. I've only been gone a couple of hours and already you've tried to burn down the shed. And it looks like a bomb has gone off in the house. You both need to help Ma'ma more. Tell me, how is school going? You start again soon."

"Do we have to go back? It is dull, and our teacher is grumpy. Grey-Kaye is a grunter.

"That is Mr Kaye from you."

"Yeah well, I understand Loin Chops better than him."

"Loin Chops? What happened to Bacon Rashers?"

"Bacon," said Jimmy matter-of-factly, as he started peeling off his wet clothes on the verandah down to his jocks.

"Oh. Okay." She smiled. The manner of naming their pigs was a family tradition. "Well, go on... put on some dry clothes. Don't forget to hang out your wet things Jimmy! Joe and I will feed the chooks and collect the eggs before we go in." Ahh. There, in the middle of the chook pen, was the truant saucepan. She picked it up and filled it with eggs from the nesting boxes.

After they came inside, Faith washed the saucepan and mixed a batch of scones, while the kids sat up at the table. She proceeded to beat a sense of order into the kitchen until she was able to poke a loaded plate of hot steaming scones towards them. Afterwards she went and sat with her mother who was bottle feeding the baby on the lounge. Faith sat, perching on a chair, with an eye on the children. "How long are these kids staying with you Ma'ma?"

"This is little Edith-Rose and that is Gus. We'll probably have them a while. Their mother has been taken to the asylum in the city. Their family is not too interested or helpful. Where is Daisy?"

"Not sure. Haven't seen her."

"No bother, she'll be in a corner reading no doubt."

"I'll start dinner for you. I am going to stay in town tonight... at Nonni Trimboli's house."

"Oh. I thought Gabe was..."

"Yeah, I saw him. I asked if I could stay there. He is doing it up."

"And you are okay with that?"

"Sure. It's their house. They can do what they want with it."

"No, I meant that..."

"Ma'ma, I know you need all the space you can find here and staying there will be convenient. It's not far. I'm going in this afternoon. I'll pack something light for dinner, and then I'll get some supplies tomorrow. I've got a list of things to organise for the wedding, so hopefully I will be able to work on ticking off those things pretty quickly in the mornings, and I'll come out for lunch and do some stuff around the house and help you get sorted for dinner... and I've some marking I have to do in the evenings as well...." She lined up potatoes on a tray and slid them into the oven for roasting. Then she extracted Daisy from her corner to peel the carrots and turnips, and enlisted Violet to start stringing beans.

Faith left soon after so she wouldn't be caught in the dark. She drove the old farm jalopy, and it chugged to a stop outside Nonni's place. She looked at the house, standing elegantly in the muted evening light. It didn't seem right that she would no longer be welcomed by Nonni's generous arms and generous heart. She almost didn't want to go inside. Perhaps her memories would stay untainted if she didn't see the house empty or witness Gabe stripping back chipped windowsills. Part of her in that moment wanted to stay looking at the house, the way she remembered it... before night fell... before the house would be shrouded in darkness without Nonni's lamp perpetually shining through the coloured glass window panel beside the front door.

Just then the light flickered on inside, and the lamp shone in the entry window, just as it had always done. She gasped, and shook her head, holding her breath. She closed her eyes. Was it possible to want something so badly, that you hallucinate? Or did Nonni live on, as her superstitious friends believed? Tears leaked out past her lashes. She opened her eyes and swiped at them quickly as Gabe strode towards her. He leant through the passenger window, relaxed in his grubby work overalls. "Are you planning on camping out here on the street? Grab your things and I'll park the ute around the back in the shed for you."

"You stayed to meet me?"

"Just wanted Nonni's lamp to welcome you one more time. And I didn't want you freaking out... being in the house of a recently departed. Us Italians are a superstitious lot."

She grinned sheepishly. "Hmm. You do remember that I am not Italian nor superstitious. And if your family is guided by such, you would be the only one to admit it."

"I disagree... you are family. But I confess I am here to reassure myself that you will be okay."

"I will be okay. And you don't have to stay."

"Well, I do really. Mamma gave my bed away."

"She gave away your *bed*?"

He laughed. "Yes... to Cousin Mirabella. Only she is not actually my cousin... well possibly a very distant cousin. She's stayed on since the funeral... and she will be here indefinitely it seems. I am fairly certain Mamma has a plan to hitch us together."

"Mirabella sounds like a pretty name for a wife."

"There you go, bringing up the name thing again. Why won't you let that go?" he asked with a grin.

"I'll remind you, that it was *your* conviction that you could never marry someone named Faith. Not Italian enough."

"Well, I was thirteen years old at the time. And you were eleven. You haven't changed your name, and I haven't changed mine. So, I think we are still at an impasse."

"The fact remains, I got in first." She got out hooking her handbag over her arm and collecting the paper bag of cut sandwiches from the passenger seat. "Thank you, for letting me stay. But... are you really planning on staying here tonight?"

"There are plenty of rooms that Nonni used for boarders. I'll take one of those since I've put you in the main. Couldn't displace a paying tenant," Gabe said, as he retrieved her suitcases from the back of the ute.

"You said I didn't have to pay."

"Actually, we agreed you would cook meals as tariff. And yet all I see is a very skimpy packed lunch, which I assume is our dinner."

"Oh. You were serious."

"Hmm. I was. I pre-empted the lack of weight you would give to our contract. So instead of going hungry tonight, I brought food you can cook," he said as he opened the door at the top of the stairs and ushered her inside. He indicated an array of pantry items on the table.

"You really want me to cook your dinner?" she asked sceptically. "Your mother cooks enough food for an army. She can't have changed that much."

"A meal is a fair exchange for a bed," he said, putting down her suitcases. "I'll move the ute, while you make dinner. I've already lit the stove." He didn't wait for a response and went outside.

She shook her head. In all truth, it was a relief – not being here alone. Growing up, cooking at Nonni Trimboli's kitchen table, was an apprenticeship in life. How many hours had she spent here... chopping and kneading and mixing and rolling and bottling, while her mother was busy with babies? She looked at the things Gabe had gathered: pasta, tomatoes, onions and eggplant. Very Mediterranean. She went outside and picked some basil from the herb garden. She scanned the pantry for the familiar corked bottle of olive oil with the medicinal dispensary label. It seemed strange that Nonni could only buy olive oil from the chemist, when she used it in all her cooking. She pulled a few cloves of garlic from the string of knobs hanging by the window. Suddenly it felt homely again.

When he came inside, Gabe perched on a stool while she cooked. He poured himself a cup from the coffeepot Faith placed on the trivet. She pushed a chopping board towards him with the bowl of tomatoes, and he sat there chopping, relaxed, talking about his plans. He wanted to repaint the entire house; redo all the casement windows; enclose part of the back verandah to update the bathroom.

"Renovated bathroom? Sounds modern."

He shrugged. "That's the idea. I'll update the kitchen too."

"But this kitchen has worked perfectly for your grandmother ever since I've known her. Why would you want to fix something that isn't broken?"

"It's worn-out and shabby like the rest of it. The tiles are falling off. Besides, no one else has the emotional attachment to this place that you and I have. A kitchen is a significant selling point in a house."

"Oh, please keep its old-world charm! I always thought Nonni's front door was like this magical portal into an authentic Italian villa. Made even more mysterious because on the outside it just looks like every other house in this very ordinary Aussie Street in our very ordinary Aussie town. Well, apart from the figurines in the front garden... which I hope you also keep."

"How would you even know? You have no idea what an authentic Italian villa might actually look like."

"Not true! Nonni showed me photos of her old home growing up. And I have access to many remarkable libraries. Art History has meant I am a familiar visitor to the literary Italian sector. Come on Gabe, you're the one who used to tell me you have responsibilities to your continental heritage."

"I'm amused by the idea that you are advocating I preserve my heritage, when as soon as you could, you ran a mile from it. But seriously, I need to consider what is practically marketable. Being Italian is not respected anywhere but in Italy... and certainly not here. The recovery agenda from the war, is encouraging more and more families to come out. But the Trimboli family was here long before this particular immigration wave was promoted. That means I am born and bred Australian."

"Nonni was remarkable in the way she was so loyal to both places." For some reason Faith teared up. Did she even have any right to grieve Nonni Trimboli at all? Nonni wasn't her grandmother. "Oh Gabe. I'm so sorry I didn't get back for the funeral. I tried, but by the time I organised my leave... and the train timetable... I just couldn't make it back in time. I miss her so much!"

"Being at the funeral wouldn't stop you missing her. I know... because I was there, and it still feels like my heart has been ripped out."

"But I wish... I wish..."

He stood up and went around the bench and held her while she sobbed into his shirt. "Nonni knew you loved her well. She did..." he murmured quietly.

* * *

3.

When Faith emerged in the morning Gabe was in his work clothes, coming in and out of one the spare rooms. The stove was already stoked and there were eggs in the basket on the bench. Gabe was stacking wooden tea-chests in the living area. "What are you doing?" she asked with a sleepy yawn.

"Packing up."

"Packing? It is barely light." She had not slept well. It was harder than she thought – trying to wind down the noise in her head.

"Yes. Packing. Family offered to do it, but if I let them in here, they will be here for six months trying to decide who will have Nonni's doilies and who will have her shoes. So, I've elected to box it all up – one room at a time and they can sort it out at home."

Faith went to the stove and put on the kettle. She turned around and looked at Gabe. He seemed like a man with a plan. Certain and decisive. What happened to the kid who couldn't decide if he even wanted to do carpentry after school?

"The stuff I want to keep I will put to the side and see if anyone actually misses it. Is there anything that you would like?"

"Gabe! You just can't give away things that belonged to your grandmother."

"Well, pretty sure she would like you to have something of hers. A keepsake... a memento."

"Well sure... that would be nice."

"She had some trinkets. Things that I don't think were expensive... but they were hers..." He brought out a box and opened the lid, tipping out the contents onto the table. There were brooches with bits of coloured glass missing from the clasps; broken strings of beads; old brooches and buttons. He rifled through it and shrugged. "I doubt there is anything of value here. I think this stuff would just go to the kids to play with. Makes good treasure for pirate games. Perhaps there is a bowl or a platter you would prefer."

"I really like that platter with the eggplants, onions and tomatoes painted on it."

"Yours," he said decisively, and went to the kitchen sideboard and pulled it out. He put it on the bench. There was a chip on the edge.

"If you are sure..."

"I know Mamma wouldn't miss it. It has sentimental value only."

Faith picked up a small brooch from the pile on the table and turned it over. The pin on the back was broken. "I remember this..." She closed her eyes. She was transported back to a Sunday morning on one of their stayover weekends. Nonni was dressing Daisy ready for church, putting shoes on her thick stockinged feet. Faith had come in with the brooch. She admired the lady on the cameo and pointed out a scratch on surface of her face. "She looks so elegant," Faith had observed. "It is a shame that little mark spoils it."

Nonni Trimboli inspected the brooch, but instead of being disappointed it wasn't perfect, she had smiled and said, "Oh, she is very elegant, little Faith. But scratches don't take away our elegance. They add character. Just be sure you choose a man who appreciates your marks and doesn't just chip away at your good nature." And then she pinned it on the hair ribbon that she had used to tie up her braid.

Gabe laughed. "Trust Nonni, to make a cameo a life lesson moment."

Faith smiled as she looked at it. "That moment transported me into womanhood. I felt so grown up. I think this elegant lady embedded my love of the classics. That moment inspired me to study art history and teach others to appreciate the beauty in things gone by. What if we could see something of that art reflected in ourselves? Even the scratches become part of the masterpiece... a flaw that adds to the beauty... much like the marble grain in the sculpture of Michelangelo's David. Other sculptors rejected that block of marble because they said nothing beautiful could be made from it due to its flaws."

Gabe pressed the cameo into her hand. "I can't think of any other person Nonni would want to have this. It needs to stay with you."

"You know, Nonni, was my strongest advocate. She made me promise that I would not give up, and that I would never settle."

"Settle?"

"Well, you know... give up on the dream, and just stay here in Lenwick and marry some farmer."

"Farmer? Which farmer?"

"Not a literal farmer... more a metaphorical farmer. You know... just anyone."

"Oh. And your banker... that's not settling? Not a professor – educating the ignorant. Not a doctor – healing the sick. Or even a farmer – feeding the hungry. But a banker... lining his pockets." He stared at her defiantly. "You said he was accomplished... that's a triumph for a banker, given what we have all just pulled through," he said sarcastically. "Faith, I didn't take you for someone who would be moved by the superficial!"

"Gabe Trimboli, I don't think you are the person to be lecturing me about what is superficial."

"Well, I don't know about that. It seems clear enough that you believe shallow would be my speciality. That, at least, gives me leave to speak to it. After all... just a chippy!"

"Don't presume to put words in my mouth Gabe Trimboli!"

"I don't believe there was any presumption. What you are thinking is pretty obvious to me!"

"Huh!" and she stormed off to her room. Then she turned around and came back and grabbed the platter and cameo off the table. "For Nonni!" she flung back as she went into her room and slammed the door."

"Well, that is really grown-up of you Faith!"

"Go away and leave me alone!" she yelled through the door.

"You want *me* to leave?"

"Yes! Leave! Go!"

"I live here!! This is my house!" He flung back at her. Then he paused and swallowed, and poured himself a coffee, hoping that perhaps Faith would not notice that particular slip.

After a short time, the door opened, and Faith appeared silently in the bedroom doorway. "You said you were working on it for your father and uncle. I thought you are renovating Nonni's house to prepare it for sale for them," she said quietly.

"I am. Sort of." There was another long pause. "Well okay. I am the one who is going to buy it. They have agreed. I want to do it up. I haven't decided definitely that I will sell it on."

Faith stared at him severely and then turned around and went back into the bedroom.

Gabe came and stood by the door, coffee mug in hand. "What are you doing?"

"I am leaving," she said packing her suitcase on the bed. "I cannot stay here if this is *your* house. I understood you were staying for one night. Or perhaps two. To accommodate Cousin Mirabella."

He shrugged and turned away. "Want breakfast before you go?" he asked as she put her suitcases by the door. She took a breath. Gabe was the most infuriating person in her life. And that was saying something. "Coffee?" he asked casually.

She nodded. She knew this was his apology. At least he let things go quickly. Worsley would have batten down the hatches for days if this had been their altercation. When it came down to an argument with Worsley, it was better to quickly concede with a white flag than to be honest about what she was thinking or feeling... on any issue. It wasn't worth the emotional siege that came afterwards. She frowned. She knew how to keep the peace with Worsley. That is what made it safe. But Gabe... she never could. It had always been like this. These two men were complete contrasts. Gabe was blustery, warm, big hearted. Worsley was firm, predictable, dashing.

Gabe put the pan on the stove. Faith stood up and took over. "I am not letting you burn my breakfast. Nonni told me that you can make anything you set your mind to, as long as it does not involve a frying pan."

"She said that? The lack of loyalty is shattering."

"Family can be ruthless in its honesty. And being ruthlessly honest Gabe, I want to assure you I am not settling. You haven't even met Worsley."

He smiled at that, as he sat down and drank his coffee. So, she considered him family. "No, I haven't met your Mr Jones. But I do know you have been on a lifelong mission to find your Renaissance Man. Perhaps this Jones is him. Or perhaps you just want him to be, and he is actually as veneered as he sounds... with nothing solid underneath the surface."

"Renaissance Man? That's ridiculous. I have never said such a thing."

"It's true. Renaissance Man. You may not have coined the term, but you have been looking for your Michelangelo marble statue your entire life. You want a perfectly sculptured King David. A man straight out of the pages of your Bible. You want a practical, down-to-earth shepherd. A courageous warrior, a fighter, a champion who conquers Goliaths. A poet and an artist. A passionate lover. A statesman forging culture and identity. A man whose spirituality is as much a part of his life as breathing. Faith, it is an impossible standard to live up to."

She looked shocked, and then laughed. "Remember when I told you Willy Stewart was the one?" She quickly sobered, sighed and shook her head. She heard Willy never came home from the war.

"I remember when, the very next week, he broke out in acne all over his face. You were devastated since David could not possibly have pimples. Faith, even if you still believe there is a real-life David out there for you, you cannot tell me this War-lord guy even comes close to your ideal. You said Nonni spoke about not settling. If you ask me, I reckon you already have."

"Well, I didn't ask you! I've already told you I am not settling! Why would you even say that?"

"Because you only mention him to defend his achievements. You never just talk about him with that glow you get. You were more in love with Willy Stewart than how you talk about Jones. There's got to be more to your relationship than his job. By that measure, you were more in love with Nonni than him."

"That's completely different. Nonni is Nonni. I have grown up now. And for your information Worsley has many wonderful qualities. He is educated. Attentive. Ambitious. Respected. And handsome."

"See. Why is handsome even on the list? It is very unlike you."

"Because Gabe Trimboli, you think you have exclusive claims on good looking. Girls have been swooning over you since grade one. We both know it."

He grinned. And drank his coffee.

"See! You do know it," she said as she flipped the fried bread and served out their eggs.

He shrugged. "And yet you are immune to me. Good looking means nothing to you really. So why bring it up? It doesn't make this guy your David."

"Gabe? Are you jealous?"

He grinned. "Fiercely. The man is marrying my very good friend. And there is no possible way he understands his good fortune. I loathe the idea he is taking you for granted."

"Huh. Well, I could say the same for Brindabella."

"Mirabella. Ahh yes. The vast and many qualities of Mirabella. She is pretty and sweet, has a great wardrobe, is an excellent cook... and she agrees with everything I say."

"Grief! That sounds intolerable!"

"And there is no possible way I am going to marry her."

"Oh... I don't know. If your mother has set Mirabella in her sights as her future daughter-in-law, do you really have a choice? Your family can be very convincing."

"My mother is not going to choose my bride. If I have to live with her, I should get a say."

"That's very modern of you Gabe... and not very Italian."

"You seem to forget I was born here. I am as Australian as you."

"Except for the Italian family... and the Italian name... and the Italian... everything."

"Well, like I said, Renaissance Man. I hope you do realise that it is an Italian initiative. We invented the idea. One hundred percent."

* * *

4.

They were washing up the breakfast dishes when there was a flurry of activity on the front verandah. Gabe looked at Faith and sighed. "Brace yourself. It is about to start."

"What is?"

"Mirabella."

"What exactly does that..."

The door opened and in gushed Gabe's mother. "Gabriele! Good morning figlio mio!"

"'Morning Mamma."

"I brought over some... Oh. You have a visitor."

"Mamma, you remember Faith. Faith Galloway."

"Good morning, Mrs Trimboli. How are you this morning?"

"Hmm. Well enough. Gabriele? What are you doing with a woman in Nonni's house? How could you disrespect her so?"

"No disrespect Mamma. Faith knew Nonni well."

"Mrs Trimboli, I am truly sorry for your loss. I..."

"Our family. Our loss. What are you doing here?" She stared at the suitcases packed by the door. "Surely you are not planning on staying?"

"Actually I..."

"This is outrageous! She cannot stay here. Nonni will be turning over in her grave, and she will never rest when it is so freshly turned!"

"Mamma. Faith has been around our family since... forever. It is like having family visit."

"But she is not family. And she cannot stay."

Faith watched as a young woman wandered through the door behind Gabe's mother and looked listlessly at various nick-nacks in the room. Her filmy dress flowed around her like a halo; it's low neckline, elegantly drawing attention to her womanly wares. This Mirabella had all the appearance of some sort of mystical Roman goddess captured by the master artists. Her dark hair and features were classic, and her lips were painted in a full-bodied rouge gloss. To Faith, Mirabella created a picture that was the personification of timeless beauty. How many artists had tried to capture on canvas what was walking around in Nonni's living room? "Pretty", Gabe had said, yet this woman was not pretty; she was classically stunning. Faith swallowed, and her curiosity stirred. Could Gabe really be impervious to her charms?

Gabe nodded to her politely. "Good morning Mirabella," he said with an unimpressed twist on his mouth. "Let me introduce you to an old friend, Faith."

Mirabella's eyes lifted in limpid pools of loveliness. "Good mornin', Gabriele," she said in a thick Italian accent.

The picture in Faith's head came crashing down like a house of cards. Her voice had none of the continental romantic lilts, but grated harshly, like fingernails down a blackboard. Faith's eyebrows shot up in shock and she quickly turned away as she was scarcely able to supress a gasp of disappointment. She glanced at Gabe who studied the basket of almond biscotti that his mother had placed on the table. He picked up a biscuit and focused on pouring another cup of coffee to accompany it.

Mirabella said something else. Faith realised that even though Mirabella was speaking, she hadn't actually heard anything she said. It would be a relief if beauties like Mirabella Rossi could swan around like those old-fashioned silent black and white movies. Faith took a deep breath and resolved something in her mind. "Mrs Trimboli, I do understand it might seem unnecessarily generous of Gabe to allow me to rent a room. But I specifically asked him to consider this, as I am here on a short leave. My fiancé is away on a business trip. I wanted to use the time to organise some of my wedding matters and catch up with my family as well. However, you know there is no space at home while my mother is looking after foster children. Here is so close to home, so I can pop out there to help Ma'ma. It's quiet, and I need to finish marking papers before I go back to start the new term."

"You *rented* the room to her?"

Gabe collaborated with a nod. "Business."

"And you are here to work?" she said, staring at Faith severely.

Faith nodded. "I have many end-term papers to grade."

"And you are really engaged?"

"Oh yes." Faith pushed forward her left hand and showed the generous rock on her finger. Mirabella stared at it lustfully. "My fiancé's name is Worsley Jones. He is *very* handsome, and a *very* well establish accountant."

"Humph." Suddenly Mrs Trimboli felt torn. That this woman was not interested in her youngest son was both insulting and a relief at the same time.

Faith took a breath. "And... here's another thought. If Mirabella was to start calling... as a single woman... it might be beneficial to have another independent person... one who is already spoken for... to be around, while Gabe is working on the house."

"*Si*. You are right. The need for a chaperone is an old-fashioned notion to some, but it is a very good idea. Not that Mirabella will have a lot of time to just come visiting and socialising. She is a very busy woman herself."

Mirabella looked up, and yawned, and said something inane that defied the claims to her demanding commitments of industry. Yet again. If only she had stayed quiet.

"Oh, I admire diligence very much. If the war did show us one thing, it is that women can hold down any job and keep a country running. The women's rights movement is gaining momentum, to bring us in line with the rest of our country's workforce. 'Equal pay for equal work' is not just a slogan, it is a completely justified principle."

Gabe's mother looked at Faith suspiciously. "So you are one of these modern types who want to stir up trouble... degrading women by forcing them to work like coal-mules?"

Faith raised her eyebrows high. "How could everything we accomplished during the war, be pushed aside as if it never happened? My father insisted that it wasn't just political freedoms that we were fighting for. It is now proven that women are capable of holding more than the unskilled jobs by keeping a nation afloat while our men went off to war. Without a doubt women can learn any job and accomplish any task – even highly skills roles. Yet it appears we are expected to go back to all the unskilled places without so much as a frown. The idea that women cannot possibly make an ongoing intelligent contribution in the workforce is not right." She mentally conceded that the notion may have merit for Mirabella, who fitted very nicely into an ornamental role.

Gabe quickly spoke up. "Mamma, did you know that Faith went to University and also Teacher's College while she was away?"

"And how does that help you cook and wash dishes?"

Faith looked at the tea-towel still in her hand and put it down quickly. No point getting into her arts degree. She wished Gabe hadn't brought that up. "I have been teaching... at a private school... the Ensley Ladies' Academy. We had to move when the school campus was seconded by the military, but we are functioning with a full cohort again. I also tutor some of the student-teachers, supporting them in their studies. Teachers are in short supply."

"You tutor student-teachers? That is hardly appropriate."

"Why ever not?"

"Teachers should be men. And a woman should not teach them. It is very clear in the Holy Book."

"Oh? How is it that we allow women to give birth, teach language, social manners, Sunday School and all sorts of subjects in Infant's School. And then one birthday comes around, but which birthday... it is not clear, but suddenly it becomes inappropriate to teach. It does not make sense. Besides, most of the students enrolled are women."

"Humph," she said unimpressed. "You're still an argumentative type – just like your mother, aren't you? Well, don't interrupt my son with his work. We have a full week to deal with, so we probably won't see much of you. Are these boxes ready to go? Gabriele, load them up and we will take them out of your way." She turned on her heel.

"Yes, good idea Mamma," and Gabe quickly picked up a box and took it outside. He finished loading and brought back some empty boxes, stacking them in the corner.

When they had gone, Gabe sat at the table and ran his hand over the back of his neck. "I need a coffee."

Faith nodded and sat beside him with the pot ready in hand. "I agree. Three cups so early in the morning is hardly enough."

"So, what happened to you not being able to stay?" he said with a dazed shake of his head.

"I just witnessed my good friend being invaded, attacked in the trenches of family expectations. I may not be here for long, but while I am, I refuse to leave you alone under this onslaught of matrimonial shellfire. I have always been your ally Gabriele Trimboli, so I am staying as reinforcements."

He reached out and pressed her hand in his. "Thank you, Faith. I've done war, and the battle comparison is not too far from the truth. Thank you. I mean that sincerely. Every time she speaks, I want to throw something."

"But she is so beautiful!"

"Yes. But you may not have noticed that look in her eye she gets when she doesn't get her own way. Amplify that over twenty years... and I am doomed. I won't do it. I can't."

Faith laughed. "So, if I am committed to my ideal of a Renaissance David... it seems you also have a flawless archetype that has captured your attention. What would that be?"

"Doesn't have to be flawless... just kind and intelligent... a woman of faith. And someone who doesn't sound like a sawmill every time she speaks. That would cover it." Bingo. He took a swallow of coffee and looked away.

"Oh, my goodness, you are after a Proverbs 31 wife... *'her price is far above rubies.'* You want a Ruby Girl! You have judged me so harshly for my aspirations, and yet, here you are, as starry eyed and idyllic as myself."

"Huh. How about that? It seems we are still two of a kind."

"All your lecturing, Gabe Trimboli, yet I have uncovered the truth once again. You cannot hide from me. I will always find you out."

"That is something our friendship has always been. We see the truth in each other Faith Galloway ... even when it is rough, and scratched, and unpolished," he looked at her and swallowed... a woman of faith. "Just like your slab of marble. Even with its flaws across the surface, one person saw the potential to form a priceless sculpture under the right master's hand."

She raised her mug in a salute. "Then, here is to the honest quest for our soul mates. To marble and gemstones in the rough." She smiled as they clinked their coffee cups. "Both are treasures," Faith said, "just like my little chipped cameo." Well, she thought, if nothing else, her holiday just became more interesting than cooking meals for rent, changing nappies, collecting eggs, supervising siblings, and marking papers.

It wasn't until much later that she realised she had completely forgotten the whole wedding planning aspect of this visit. So, in a frenzy of guilt, she spent hours working on a guestlist to send out wedding invitations.

* * *

Every morning, Mirabella made an appearance. Regardless of Mrs Trimboli's assertion that their schedule was full, Mirabella sat around listlessly, looking like an Italian fashion model straight from the pages of Grazia Magazine. She flaunted her tiny waistline that was highlighted by her modern wardrobe. She flashed her eyelashes in time with her elegant boredom as if on a catwalk parading every ensemble, preening and pouting in alternating cycles. Gabe became furiously immersed in scraping back paint, or weeding the garden, or cleaning out the gutters. Basically, anything to stay out of her way. Although Mirabella did not give up visiting, she generally wearied of being ignored and vowed she would come again tomorrow in the hope that Gabe's schedule would miraculously open up. To Mirabella's credit, she always returned, in another glamorous outfit that might capture his attention. And yet his frenzied work never abated.

During these visits, while Gabe was busy evading Mirabella, Faith attempted to engage her in conversation. Mirabella always had a copy of Grazia or Lei magazine in her hand, and happily relayed a tale of some turned head, or a flattering comment she encountered that day. She would count the number of generous bouquets that were offered to her by gentlemen around town. Whenever Faith tried to redirect the conversation to something she considered a little more meaningful, Mirabella's eyes would glaze over and talk about food. Faith quickly recognised the topics that had Mirabella yawning. Issues that promoted equality for young women, not just in education but in all sorts of professional pathways, including political representation, had her flipping the pages of her magazines in a flurry. They were printed in Italian and her only response was to insist that fashion was infinitely more useful. "I can get any door opened, just by being woman," she said in her thick accent. "I don't need a certificate for that – just a very pretty, well-cut dress," Mirabella said, turning another page and adjusting her bustline with a knowing smile and a raised brow.

Faith gagged. Perhaps the classically elegant Mirabella, did not want to be rescued from her ignorance through well-intentioned conversation. Faith had vainly hoped for parallel endearing qualities of a country work-ethic, innocence, self-improvement, and chastity. Suddenly she appreciated that Gabe's aversion for the mythical beauty of Mirabella went deeper than auditory reasons. If Gabe had made up his mind, he would never give way. Faith was grateful that she wouldn't have to insert herself into this triangle much longer. She was well and truly ready to go home.

* * *

5.

Faith sat at the table with a pile of papers at her elbow. Her time had passed quickly, and she was trying to finish this final round of marking today. She studied the essay before her with a frown. She paused before she wrote a response in the margin with her fountain pen.

"It's late. Do you think you will be stopping for lunch soon?" asked Gabe as he stacked another box by the door.

"Nearly done. Just a few more to do."

"Packing up Nonni's things is taking me much longer than I ever imagined. I've been so busy avoiding Mirabella, that the yard is looking good. But I have been messing around the packing up for a whole fortnight now. I find it impossible to do it without deliberating over every little thing, and I am still torn because I don't know the story behind her stuff. What if I throw out something important? Surely it can't be this difficult!"

Faith wiped the nib of her fountain pen, screwed on the lid and put it down. "Isn't that the point? These are not your boxes to sort. Just hand them over. You said your family would make the call about what's what and how to distribute it."

"Perhaps you're right. I am making it harder than it needs to be."

"Let's have lunch... and then I'll help you for a bit before I go out to Ma'ma's place."

"Are you sure?" He frowned and looked at the essays still to be marked.

"Don't reproach me, or I will change my mind. Besides, it will be a distraction. I've earned some head-clearing space."

Faith stacked away her work, made some lunch and a pot of coffee, and they sat together, comfortably chatting. There was a knock at the door. Faith swallowed. "Oh really? Do you think I am on Chaperone Duty again, so soon? This morning's visit dragged on forever. I can't focus on marking while she is drooling over her magazines... or staring me down. But at least I was able to do some cleaning for you."

"I would prefer if you didn't call it Chaperone Duty," he said, "It implies her invasion has potential to progress to treaty. I'll remind you this will always be a dead-end street." He got up to answer the door and ushered a lady into the room wearing a grim suit. She looked uneasy. "Faith, do you remember Mrs Martin?"

Faith awkwardly pushed aside her plate and stood up. "Of course. Mrs Martin. Good afternoon. How is Mr Martin? And Levi and Robert? I trust they are both well."

The woman nodded and restlessly fiddled with her cuffs. "Levi finished his apprenticeship at the printers since being discharged. He's home now. Robert left school. There really wasn't any point continuing. It is a shame though – I had such high hopes for him."

"Oh, I'm sorry Mrs Martin. That must be disappointing for you." Faith paused awkwardly and stood up. "Yes well, I will give you some space, so you can visit with Gabe without interruption. Can I get you a cup of tea?" Faith started to clear their lunch from the table.

"Faith, Mrs Martin has come to speak with you," clarified Gabe.

She looked up surprised. "Me?"

"Miss Galloway, I am very sorry to disturb you. I assumed lunch would be finished." She looked significantly at the clock on the mantle.

"No bother really. I became absorbed in marking papers," she said. That sounded more acceptable than the extended Chaperone Duty that disrupted her entire morning. She should have just left and gone to visit her mother at the farm.

"That is so admirable. This is why we need to talk."

"What exactly did you want to discuss?" Faith asked as they sat in the lounge surrounded by boxes. She poured a cup from the teapot. Mrs Martin sipped her tea, and then put down her cup in its saucer, anxious to start.

"Well, you know I am part of the school committee," began Mrs Martin.

"Oh dear. I did not know that. Has Jimmy or Joe been in trouble again?"

"Your brothers? No, no. Well, perhaps... but no more than any of the other children. I think they have only been sent home four or five times this term."

"Five times! That is not 'only' Mrs Martin! That is unacceptable! I apologise for their behaviour, but you must realise they have been so unsettled... since..."

"Yes, yes. I know. I am of the mind behaviour is often related to other factors."

"Oh, well, thank you for understanding. Ma'ma wants them to do well at school. You really should be talking to her about their behaviour."

"Well, that was not the purpose of my visit. There is something that specifically pertains to you." She took a breath and launched ahead. "I would like to offer you the job."

"What job?"

"The schoolteacher's job. We want you to stay on as Lenwick's teacher."

"Me? But you already have a teacher and I already have a job."

"Yes, I know. But you are from Lenwick. And you are so very well... qualified. And Mr Kaye has no idea about children. He does okay with the older students, I guess. But now we have more enrolments we need to put on another teacher, and we have been so hopeful since you have come back, that the committee asked if I would approach you to take the appointment. We can offer accommodation as part of your package." She said it in a rush and then took a deep breath as she paused.

"Mrs Martin I am only here on a holiday, and I will be leaving again soon. I am sorry but I am not in a position to take your offer."

"Please Miss Galloway... please consider it. All our children are suffering, and if you want your brothers and sisters to retrieve any sort of respectable education, then they need more than what they have now. I am sure if there had been a teacher of your calibre, Robert could have gone on to something much better. These students need more. They all do."

"And what about Mr Kaye?"

"He would retain his position. He doesn't know we are looking to appoint another teacher of course, so I would appreciate your discretion in this matter. No one must know we have talked."

Faith nodded. "Well, like I said, I am flattered, but at the moment I am not in a position to accept your kind offer. But if you like, I have other contacts who may be suitable candidates for you to consider."

"Miss Galloway... Faith... you know Lenwick. You know our children. Please... just think on it. In my mind, we haven't had a suitable teacher since, well, since Mrs James actually. Outsiders like Mr Kaye do not seem to work out. You will be doing your brothers and sisters... all of us... a huge favour."

Faith sat still like stone for a long time after Mrs Martin left. Gabe came and took away the teapot and put a cup of coffee down beside her. "Are you okay?"

She shrugged. She was not sure. "Did you hear that?"

"Some of it." He held his breath. "You said no," he observed.

"It's not practical. I have commitments: my job; my students. I have a fiancé. My life is no longer in Lenwick. There is no point trying to talk me into it." Of course Gabe would add his voice to the chorus of expectations placed on her.

He shrugged. "Why would I do that? It sounds like a backyard thing to me."

"What backyard thing?"

"Your mother told me about it."

"I don't remember her saying anything about our backyard."

"When I was finishing up school, I was so torn up about doing the right thing. There was so much tension between pleasing my family, and pleasing my teacher, and pleasing myself, and pleasing God. It seemed too much. I didn't want to step wrong... or go against God's will. But I had no idea which was which. Your mother gave me some fresh bread... and pointed out..."

"The ragged edges. Yeah, I know. That is still her mainstay life lesson."

He grinned. "True... but then she also said that she likes to think of these decisions in the same way she thinks about being a kid. She spoke about your backyard when you were living in the house next-door. There's that tree where you and Philip built a cubbyhouse. And the chook yard, and some beams around the shed that you used to balance on, and a sand pit, and a corner under the shrubs where you would go and read. She said she didn't mind what you did so long as you were safe and stayed inside the fence. And sometimes, if there was a particular thing that she wanted you kids to do, then she would call you in onto the verandah and give you a specific job. If you didn't do what she asked... that was a problem. But until then, anything you chose to do was okay."

She studied his face quietly. "And..."

"Has she never told you this? God gives us a big backyard to play in and nothing is particularly right or wrong... it's just whatever we prefer to do at the time... as long as we stay inside his moral fence. That helped me a lot. I was free to do further study if I wanted, or I could stay and do carpentry if that worked for me as well. God hadn't given me a particular direction, so I was free to play in my back yard. If this is your back yard... and God has given no particular indication one way or another... you don't have to take this job. You are free to climb another tree. Even your city job. It's okay to say no."

"I didn't expect you to be supportive of this. You surprise me Gabe."

"Well perhaps I'm growing up. Doesn't mean I won't miss you though. I like having you around. Are you going to tell your mother about the job offer?"

"Oh Gabe, even if Ma'ma told you that story, she would still want me to stay. And I feel sorry that she has so much trouble managing the kids. And it's unfortunate that the school has difficulty finding a suitable teacher... but actually, this is not my box to sort. My life is not here. Part of me wants to do it, but I can't do everything. So, no, I don't think I will tell her about it. I don't want to get her hopes up." She stood and went over and picked up a box with a bundle of newspaper. "I said I would think about it, so I'll do that. I'll write to Mrs Martin and definitely give her my decision when I get back to the city... but really, I already know I'm not in a position to help."

He followed her into the room. Faith lined up some boxes along the bed. "Let's clear a room for you," she said decisively. "Pass me things and I'll wrap and stack in these boxes."

"Alright then!" They found a rhythm and the cupboards and shelves started to empty. The pictures on the wall came down. Gabe kept the floormat and the washstand, but other than that the room looked remarkably empty in a very short time. No frilly doilies, no cushions on the bed, no candelabras standing in the corner. Without pausing they moved into the main bedroom. Faith packed her files and things to the side, and they gave that room the same treatment.

It was focused, purposeful, and... wonderful. Keeping in step like that, like partners on a dance floor. Faith always thought that was what partners did in life too. There was none of the sparring that was her usual pattern with Gabe. She frowned as she realised that they had not argued the entire afternoon. Not once. At all.

Her frown deepened as she tried to recall a time when she had worked on a project with Worsley like this. When did they even have opportunities to create the rhythm that she had with Gabe? Their jobs... their lives... were so diverse. They needed to discover different ways where they could find that synchronised dance rhythm. Hmm.

Faith went out to the farm to say goodbye to her family. She didn't stay long because the train left early in the morning. Gabe took the packed boxes over to his parent's place and Faith started to prepare dinner while he was gone. She smiled, as she chopped the tomatoes and onions and stirred them into the Bolognese sauce... and imagined packing boxes with Worsley. Yes. She needed to go back home to the city and find those places that represented their together life.

When Gabe returned, Faith already had her things packed up. He looked at them with a sigh. "You're going tomorrow."

She nodded. "I am."

"Well, we both knew that was coming... so let's just enjoy our last evening together. Next time you come to visit, no doubt it will be to make a promise to be Mrs Jones. Your mother said you had settled on a date."

"There really wasn't much choice. It depended on when the church was available during school breaks. I always said this visit was a short one. Although your mother will be particularly content to see me gone. And Mirabella will also be relieved since I am the competition."

He laughed. "There is no competition. But if there was... you would win, hands down. So, no need to feel insecure. Apart from my rather defensive family, be reassured Faith Galloway... you are loved. I'd be happy enough to see you stay." His eyes connected with hers and there was a pause.

She nodded. "Yes, I know. I have always known," she said softly.

He cleared his throat. "Yes well. So, what will our farewell evening look like. After dinner what would you like to do?"

"This sounds silly, but I want to help you finish your boxes. Then you can get in and properly start work on the house."

"Doesn't that seem like a waste? We could go out..."

"And be accosted by any number of well-meaning locals who want to see me embedded here until my feet are fossilised in local Lenwick soil? I'd rather be here with you."

"Faith Galloway makes the closing argument with convincing clarity. Are you sure you didn't study to be a Barrister?"

"Your rebuttal abilities were not too shabby. Don't dismiss your own particular skillset Gabe Trimboli."

"I don't. Debating aside, I keep in mind that Jesus was a carpenter. That sometimes helps. He wasn't above it."

"Oh Gabe, you have so much capacity. Don't you feel that woodwork is a waste of your talent?"

"Huh. And I've just observed it was the profession of choice for the Son of God! But I do sometimes wonder what it would have been like if I had been more determined to pursue a career like yourself. Guess I just didn't have the motivation to fight for it like you did. Still, I know nothing's wasted, but I admit... I folded. I know it. I wanted to climb the tree, but it seemed too intimidating, so I just stayed in the sandpit. And then I was called up. Literally. Not by God... but the army... and I had to leave." He shrugged. "I guess coming back has made me realise Lenwick is home. I don't want to leave now. I did that... and it wasn't good."

"So, you think you would you never leave Lenwick again... at all?"

"I doubt it. Coming back meant I had to work out what this job offers me, aside from income. I get to stay in my hometown. Carpentry is something I don't mind. I've developed practical skills in a trade. I like working with wood and with people. The people side was something that Old Henrik was never great at. I still keep an eye on him. The war was hard on him, just as much as anyone. Since he's been released from the prison-camp, he's been working from his garage. People have still painted swastikas over his door. It upsets him so much. He hasn't got a Nazi bone in his body. It doesn't seem to matter that he's been in this region longer than most. Certainly, he was here long before Hitler ever hit the radar. All that to say, carpentry ticks a few boxes for me, so that in the end it was a fair option." He paused and looked at her straining the pasta for their dinner. "So Lenwick is my sandpit. I'm happy. What does your tree-climbing do for you?"

"The students. I love my students. I love seeing their learning and their enthusiasm and their drive. I love seeing the light switch on in their eyes when they suddenly understand something. And although I miss home, I love the energy of living in the city, and the people I meet."

"All positive things..."

"Don't say it..." she said with a shake of her head.

"Say what?"

"That the job here, would offer all those benefits as well. That I wouldn't be short-changed by coming back here and taking the job at Lenwick school."

"I didn't say it. Seems I didn't need to."

"But it doesn't offer Worsley. He would never leave the city, just like you would never leave here. That is a non-negotiable for me." She threw it out there... to see if he would bite as she finished setting the table.

But tonight was their last night together and Gabe was determined not to snap at any bait. Instead, he grinned as they sat down to eat. "What sort of name is Worsley anyway?"

She chuckled and shook her head. "Apparently his parents needed to try something interesting... to go with Jones."

"You've got to admit, it sounds like a disease. That's what you have: Worsley Syndrome. Perhaps you should get Philip to check him out... see if he's contagious."

"Philip has already diagnosed him as being pathologically ambitious. I'd prefer Philip's medical degree be put to proper use to deal with real illnesses, rather than worrying about some ailment you've made up because you disapprove of his success."

He laughed. "Philip says that? Huh. There is some relief knowing that your brother thinks this guy is unexpected for you. Perhaps Dr Mortimer's famous Tonic would do your Worsley Jones some good."

Faith changed the subject. "Let's tackle the linen press... and then the kitchen."

"I am going to take full advantage of your services. Any advice on what might be useful for a bachelor-basic household is welcome. Everything else goes."

* * *

6.

Faith walked across the platform and boarded the train, making her way through to the 'Ladies Only' carriage. She was relieved that the compartment was empty, and she pulled out a book to read so she could be immersed in it before anyone arrived to attempt conversation. She looked out the carriage window and watched a few families and friends waving goodbye to passengers. The train hissed and plunged the platform in a cloud as it pulled out. The steam cleared, and she caught sight of Gabe standing there. She frowned slightly as he tipped his hat in farewell. She had not expected him to stay until the train left. As she raised her gloved hand and nodded to him, a sudden wave of sadness shrouded her eyes. He turned to go, and it seemed to mark a change. Again. Things were always changing. Just now she wanted to wind back the clock on her mother's mantlepiece and have things stay the same a little longer. It seemed a strange thing to wish for, given that she considered herself a woman of progress.

Well, in this changing world, at least Worsley was a symbol of stability. They kept to the same routines; they had the same friends; they held the same tastes in furniture as they were preparing to set up their home. Actually, the type of furnishings Worsley chose were not really to her taste, she decided. Working in Nonni Trimboli's kitchen again, made her realise that country-home was more her style. She frowned. She had never actually identified that before, but it didn't matter, so long as they were together. She knew that this last look at Lenwick, as the train wound its way out of town, was closing a chapter. It was ushering in another change. Gabe was right. Next time she returned it would be to become Mrs Jones. Her insistence on holding to the tradition of having the wedding in the bride's hometown had seemed unreasonable to Worsley. His argument for a modern, educated woman not being bound by such traditions made sense. But it was not just about the tradition. Of course, she had to consider her family. With the animals they could not up and go for a week. She sighed. Worsley would never be seen sitting on the dairy stool in the shed milking a cow, or fixing a hole in the fence like Gabe, or chopping tomatoes in Nonni's kitchen with her. No, that was her past, and her visits to Lenwick were about to change forever.

Faith was not a selfish person. She felt the pressure of her mother's position. But at the same time, there were things her mother could do, to alleviate her situation... like, refusing to take in more children. Jimmy and Joe were a handful. They were eighteen months apart, but they were bound together in trouble like twins. And to add other children into the mix? That didn't seem reasonable. Her mother had always been logical, practical, sensible... except when it came to babies.

The job offer from the school was unexpected. She sighed and put the book in her lap. She didn't attempt to read it but looked out the window. "*I am not in a position to help. Not really,*" she repeated to herself. She sighed again and looked at the gum-trees flashing passed. Every so often the train slowed to a stop. There were small sidings marked by a post with a rough sign nailed to it; sometimes there was a lean-to for shade. Parcels were dumped off, and the guard would adjust the portable step so a passenger could clamber on. Hmm. The view of the railway from this side of the city hardly seemed progressive. But she reminded herself that real progress doesn't have to be ostentatious like an elaborate railway station; it just needs to be better than it was before. She had often encouraged her students with that idea. *Better than it was before.* The railway was better for these outlying communities. Much better.

She closed her eyes and felt the sway of the carriage. There was the smell of coal smoke leaking in around the windows. The rhythmic percussion of the engine. The creak of the carriage door and the rattle of the windows. It all created a sensory backdrop to the movement of rolling forward. "Oh Lord God..." It was a prayer of the heart. She hardly knew how to articulate what she held there. The sadness of turning the page and saying goodbye to a beloved chapter was comforted by the awareness that she didn't need to wrap vocabulary or syntax around her experiences with God. He understood. He already knew the beginning and the end. All of it. For her, she was grateful this was a relationship she didn't need to navigate like peace treaties. This was more a matter of being aware... aware that God was here...holding her... and holding her loved ones, even if she wasn't in a position to help.

"Go back and teach the children. Give them twelve months." There was no sound... but there was a voice inside her head. Or was it inside her heart? Faith went still. Frozen. The book in her hand slipped to the floor. Had God just called her onto the verandah, like Gabe said? She had never heard God's Holy Spirit this distinctly. Clear. Unambiguous. Not like this. It took her breath away.

Suddenly, what had been impossible was now necessary. She had no doubt. There was no question that God had spoken, or that this was exactly what she would do. Obeying was not the question. The question was how. How would she push everything out for a year? Would Worsley understand?

As she got closer and closer to the city, Faith started to feel more and more agitated. The stations became increasingly larger, more passengers got on, and sat in her carriage. Faith understood this wasn't just about the school but supporting her mother... and not just about supporting her mother, but also her brothers and sisters as well. She instinctively knew that if she didn't want to see them derailed by life one day, then she needed to follow through because this was critical. As passengers come and went, she became afraid that she would fold. She was afraid that Worsley would not appreciate how important this was; that he would rationalise it away; that she would have to defend her faith; that she would not push through the battle of misunderstanding and do it anyway. Her agitation became more and more intense, until, at the very next stop, she grabbed her bag and disembarked. She went straight to the ticket master. "Ticket back to Lenwick Station please."

"Where? Oh, you mean Renwick?"

"No Sir. Lenwick... L-E-N-wick... out past..."

He was studying a map on the wall. "Oh. Yes. There it is. Huh. That's an out-of-the-way place for a lovely lady like yourself. This train is on the line that goes through there."

"*Not helpful,*" she thought. "*Just pass the ticket.*" She grimaced. "When does the next train go back out there, please?" she asked sweetly. With a frown.

"Huh. A bit of a wait. Two days. Half eight in the evening. Platform Two."

"I have luggage on this train that I will need taken off now or redirected. Can you organise that?" She showed him her original ticket.

That sent him into a bit of spin. But he whistled to a porter, who accosted the guard, who directed the station baggage handlers, who riffled through the luggage carriage... and soon Faith was presented with her bags. At least that was one thing.

She found a boarding house, and checked in. She went for a walk along the street and sat down in a café with a coffee. Funny how her childhood at Nonni's table had embedded a preference for Italian coffee, rather than English tea. The liquid in her cup was dark and bitter. She cringed and drank it anyway. Then she ordered a sandwich; the bread was hard, and the cheese was overly mature. In the end she just pushed it aside.

Faith started to formulate a letter to Worsley in her head, jotting notes on a paper serviette. Should her tone be apologetic when she was not sorry for doing this? How much detail should she offer in her explanation? Should she include the God factor? She didn't want to give the impression she'd had a break in reality and gone a little insane. Did it matter if he could not understand... all of it, or even just a little bit? A longer engagement was not unheard of. Afterall, she had refused to marry Worsley in a whirlwind when he came home on leave during the war. Many of her friends had done that... offering a lantern of hope for their sweethearts while they were away on active duty. That hadn't seemed so urgent since Worsley served in administration. There was so much to think about, but she realised something as she sat there drinking that bitter cup of coffee. Going back like this looked impetuous, scratched, and unwieldy on the surface, but underneath she noticed an inexplicable calm. She was very grateful for that. It gave her courage to stay firm.

Faith used her waiting time to write a letter to the college and to the Ensley Girls' Academy. She submitted an application for extended leave and posted the graded school files back to the Academy. She braced herself as she licked the stamps and handed her letter to Worsley across the counter at the post office. Sometimes he needed time to adjust, but he would eventually come around. Her family needed her. Yes. That is what she would focus on. That was the bottom line. They needed her.

* * *

7.

Faith knocked on the door. It was still dark with just the barest tinge of light starting to fade the night sky on the horizon. She knocked again. And again.

She heard him inside. A groggy voice called out. "Go away. I'm not answering the door."

She knocked again. "Gabe?"

"You heard me. Go away."

She knocked again.

"Damn it, Mirabella, I am not letting you in my house in the middle of the night, and I am not going to change my mind. You are just going to have to accept that!"

"It's Faith."

There was silence. The door unlatched and he stood there, crumpled from sleep. "What are you doing here?"

"I am going to take the job at the school."

"Huh."

"Can I come in?"

"Oh. Yes. Sure." He stepped aside, and then went and stoked the wood stove. He positioned the kettle over the plate. "Have you eaten?"

"The train-station food was disgusting, and I am past starvation. What have you got?"

"I have salami... bread... cheese. I could make you one of my sandwiches."

"That sounds infinitely better than anything I paid money for."

He sawed off a couple of slices, smothered them in some sort of sauce, sliced the salami and cheese and then whacked them in the pan, and then flipped them over until the cheese melted through. He put it on the plate with the elegance of a post hole digger shovelling dirt.

Faith ate with gusto. "Oh! It is a long time since I've had one of these. Nonni used to make them for Sunday night dinner sometimes. She was not being entirely fair when she said you could not do *anything* with a frying pan."

He sat down with a coffee and looked at her. "Faith. You're going to have to tell me what's going on. Why are you here?"

She shrugged and then told him.

He drained his cup. "So, you came back for your mother... and your brothers... because God called you in onto the verandah and told you to take the job."

She nodded. "I know. Sounds like something out of novel... or a poorly directed movie. I didn't expect this, but it happened."

"So... you and Mr Jones... no problems there?"

"Well... I don't think so. But, in all fairness Worsley doesn't know I've come back yet. I didn't even get all the way home. I have written to him. We'll just push everything out for twelve months. Longer engagements happen."

"Hmm. So still engaged. Still working at a school. Still organising your wedding."

"Yep. Everything is exactly the same... except that I'm in Lenwick for twelve months now, instead of a few weeks. Why?"

"Well. Just trying to work out if you wanted to rent the room again... whether that would be appropriate. Sounds like your circumstances are the same as before. So, you could stay here if you wanted to."

"Oh. That's a kind offer Gabe, but I am not going to stay here. They have a schoolteacher's residence. I'm just not sure how soon it will become available. I'd appreciate being able to stay until then."

He shrugged. "Sure." And he changed the subject. "Mirabella has upped the ante. She refuses to accept my 'No' is sure. Since you left, she has started telling people we are about to be engaged."

Faith's eyes went wide. "Oh Gabe! I've just been gone a few days! What are you going to do?"

"The same as I am doing now. Refute every comment, contradict every lie, counter every inuendo. Although it's not working very well. It is like I am being framed for a wedding. I'm just waiting for the time she tells everyone she is pregnant."

"Grief! Would she go that far?"

"Don't know,.. but if she does..." He shrugged. "I don't have a comeback for that. If she actually gets pregnant, I won't be able to prove the baby is not mine. I do not even think that such a scenario is beyond the realms of possibility. It would be my word against hers."

"If I stay here, will that help though? Your mother saw me as a collaborator in your courtship with Mirabella. In her mind, being on Chaperone Duty supported her mission..."

"Only because you sold it to her. Mamma still believes I will come around. But the manipulation has driven the final nail in this particular matrimonial coffin. There is no way! You know, I think this could be the thing that would make me consider leaving."

"You feel that strongly about it? Well, I expect I will be staying here at least a couple of weeks until school starts. Might be longer, but either way, let me know if you need anything, won't you? Anything at all."

"Likewise, Faith Galloway. I am here to help you settle back into Lenwick. It is good to have you home. I am relieved."

"Well, I am quite tuckered out. I am going to lie down for a couple of hours, then I will go and see Mrs Martin... and Ma'ma. Not sure what the boys will think about me being their schoolteacher. Getting them used to that idea may take more negotiating than anything the Paris Peace Treaties are undertaking. The girls will be okay with it I think." She shook her head in amazement. It was funny how things were lining up and slotting into place. That had to be a sign of the divine purpose. She wound her alarm clock and slept soundly.

* * *

Mrs Martin answered the door. "Oh Miss Galloway! You are here!" She sounded genuinely surprised, and Faith smiled.

"Yes Mrs Martin. May I come in?"

"Yes, yes... do come in. I will make some tea."

As she settled in the lounge, Faith took the teacup she was offered. "Mrs Martin, I have considered what you asked of me, and I would like to accept your offer for the new schoolteacher's position."

"Oh."

"Oh? Is the offer no longer open?"

"Well... umm... I'm sure it will be okay. When we heard you left town without a response, the committee met, and it was decided to pursue other candidates. But now that you are back... I will tell them straight away, of course."

"But we agreed I would confirm my response by letter when I arrived back in the city. We talked about that... remember? That timeframe has nowhere near expired."

"You did? Oh well, never mind. The committee was getting restless, so they felt they could not wait. But you are here now, in person, and that is good. I am very glad you didn't leave it any longer to return though. This will definitely be more convincing than a letter of interest... although if you could write one, that would be helpful... I am sure."

"Mrs Martin, was the committee on board with this appointment, or was it just your idea?"

"No, no. They were very supportive. Sort of."

"Sort of? That doesn't sound convincing. Do they want me as the schoolteacher or not?"

"Oh yes! Yes! Please Miss Galloway. This school needs you. It really does. You just write that letter, and I will manage the committee."

"So... do I have the job or not?"

"Well... I am sure that you will have it... soon. But this opportunity is not official, of course you understand, so you probably should not tell anyone about it just yet.

"Oh... Oh. Opportunity?" Faith blinked. Just a possibility. Just a chance. Not a position. Not a job. She had assumed she would be signing letters of appointment this morning. Suddenly she wavered. Did she really hear God... or was it her own imagination? All her certainty and confidence shimmered like a mirage. "I will write the letter... and please let me know as soon as you can, when it is confirmed."

Faith stood up and smoothed her skirt. Of course it would be confirmed. God said.

* * *

56

8.

Faith sat in her mother's living room and wondered how she got so carried away. She was normally very considered, rational, reasonable... yet she had taken this giant leap, and suddenly the ground was giving way underneath her. She watched the perpetual whirlwind caused by her brothers wreaking havoc in their wake in a detached sort of way. She told her mother about Mrs Martin's job offer... and the train-trip... and her conviction that God had asked her to come back and take the position... and how she had uncharacteristically turned around straight away to come back home. Her mother teared up. "Oh Faith, it means so much having you here."

"But Ma'ma, when I went to see Mrs Martin this morning, she had not exactly withdrawn the offer... but she was very uncertain about the appointment. She said I was not to tell anyone about it, until it was definite. The whole thing seems quite dodgy now. I thought I was doing the right thing. I couldn't stay on that train. I had to come back. Now it seems there is no job for me. And I've already written to the Academy and applied for extended leave."

"And there is your answer. You have done what you can. Stay with it. Don't eliminate the possibility of holding that job. You do your bit. And God will do his."

"You make it sound so simple..."

"I think it is simple: just keep going. Just do the next thing. But simple does not make it easy. Oh no... to step out in faith can be the hardest thing of all. It takes courage and strength to do that and stay sweet, my dear. That is the hardest of all."

Faith reached out and held her mother's hand. "But that is what you have done Ma'ma all your life. And you have managed to keep the kindest, sweetest heart through it all."

"It hasn't been easy with your father gone. Even though the Allies won the war, we also lost so much. I was determined not to impose restrictions on you because of that. Both you and Philip are incredible young people... and I see Daisy growing up into such a beautiful young woman as well. Violet is not far behind her. The young ones too. You all need to be able to live your own lives. I don't want my circumstances to interfere with your best possibilities."

"But Ma'ma, isn't this what family does... to be here for each other? I think I understand that better now. It's not that I didn't want to help before, I just could not see how it was possible. But obviously it was completely achievable. I just needed to say yes. And now I am here. Although I didn't expect to be here without a job... with nowhere to stay."

She finished her letter of interest explaining her qualifications, academic achievements, and experience. Then she wrote to Worsley again telling him that she had arrived safely back in Lenwick and would be staying on a little longer. Until she had the job, it didn't seem necessary to put the entire year out there. Besides, she had been instructed to keep the process confidential. She went to the post office to mail Worsley's letter and then took her application over to Mrs Martin.

"Miss Galloway, I spoke with the committee this morning and the panel would like to interview all the candidates."

"Oh. A full interview panel... in Lenwick?"

"Yes, this will demonstrate that this professional appointment is fair and reasonable."

"Oh. Well, that shouldn't be a problem. I am available at any time."

"They are interviewing another candidate today... and they can fit you in tomorrow." She wrote the time on a slip of paper.

Fit her in? Mrs Martin completely avoided the small detail that she had approached Faith and offered her this job! Fair and reasonable? The whole thing was becoming quite unreasonable. "Very well Mrs Martin. You may reassure the others on the panel that I will attend the interview at the schoolhouse. I'll see you tomorrow."

"Oh Miss Galloway," said Mrs Martin apologetically. "I am not included on the interview panel. I'm sure you understand."

* * *

Faith walked up the school stairs. Since the committee had chosen a formal process, she decided on a very practical, formal suit. She rehearsed responses to likely questions on curriculum, classroom management, educational motivation, and scholiastic rigor. She walked along the verandah to the classroom and saw three men sitting on chairs lined up in front of the classroom. They were faces she knew... long standing Lenwick names. Faith felt she was being ushered into the dock for a courtroom hearing. The men stayed seated, gesturing for her to enter. They seemed to expect she would squeeze into the student bench seats at the desks. She was certainly not going to perch on a desk in front of them. Hmm. Did she dare call them on this ridiculous omission of courtesy? Conducting the whole interview standing would be preferrable.

Faith waited wordlessly for them to offer her a seat. Mr Stewart eventually spoke. "Miss Galloway, are you not going to sit?"

"Sir? I come as a candidate for the position of teacher, not as a student. I think an 'adult' seat is only fair. Afterall, we are here as peers."

They all frowned and started jotting furiously. Apparently, the seating arrangement had been a test. Mr Martin cleared his throat and offered her his chair and then retrieved another chair from the adjoining room himself. Faith nodded and sat. "Thank you, Mr Martin. Mr Stewart. Mr Romano. I appreciate the opportunity to apply for the teacher's position."

"Well, let's get started. Tell us about yourself."

"Did you receive the letter I forwarded to you?"

"Yes of course."

"I am not sure what additional information I can offer you. You know my family. You know I grew up in Lenwick and I think this is a wonderful opportunity to sow back into the community that has offered me so much growing up. I've detailed my studies. Learning has been one of my lifelong joys and I wish to pass that love onto my students. Being a teacher has been my long-standing ambition and I have experience teaching at the Ensley Ladies' Academy, as well as..."

"Do you speak another language?" Mr Romano cut in.

"I studied Latin at college. It is the root language of the five Romance languages. I studied French at university. And I have a bit of conversational Italian."

"Latin is a dead language," Mr Romano said dismissively.

"The study of Latin is significant in achieving scholastic mastery of English," she argued.

"Hmm. What sort of practical skills do you have Miss Galloway?" asked Mr Martin, after a pause.

"Practical skills?"

"Yes practical. We want our students to have proficiency in a range of skills, not just theoretical studies. We are a rural school after all."

"Do you mean like milking a cow, or gardening... or perhaps needlepoint, cooking, or musicianship? Some outside activities, some inside. I am accomplished in all these. Would you like me to go on?"

"Dairymaid? Could you not lead with some ability that demonstrated a little more dignity?" observed Mr Stewart with a frown.

"Yet you asked for practical. People still want milk with their porridge in the morning, whether accessing that milk lacks dignity or not. I encourage my students to appreciate that every experience brings richness to a lifelong learner. My teacher, Mrs James, taught me that." Mrs James was her father's cousin, and she had spent a lot of time in their home. Whether that had been a schoolroom or a loungeroom lesson she could not be sure.

The men on the panel grunted, asked a few more random questions.

"Are you engaged to be married Miss Galloway?" asked Mr Martin staring at her left hand.

"I'm sorry? How is my private life relevant to my professional capacity to teach?"

"It is a simple enough question. It is our policy not to hire married women. So, if you are engaged, it is information that will influence your suitability for the appointment. It is a point of great relevance," said Mr Romano.

She shook her head. "Mrs James was employed here at Lenwick school. She was married."

"Yes. That was okay during the war, but I remind you she left when she became a mother. The committee made a resolution to forestall such a disruptive occurrence in the future by not employing married women. This policy enhances stability for the students' learning," explained Mr Stewart very slowly, his tone was pompous.

Faith sighed and supressed the rebuttals that sat on her tongue. When she confirmed that she was engaged, they all nodded gravely and then dismissed her like a student at the end of a school-day. Faith couldn't help noticing it was without the smile, or the word of encouragement that she always offered her students when home-bell rang. Everyone knew that married women were unemployable, and although she would not be married until after her twelve months were over, it seemed being engaged likewise disqualified her.

Faith went back to Nonni Trimboli's house, and Gabe quickly put on the coffeepot when he saw her deflated face. "So... when do you start?" he asked tentatively.

"I've attended all sorts of rigorous interviews.... for entry into university; teacher's college; a teacher's position at an elite private school for young women; and for tutoring jobs. None of those experiences prepared me for what I just endured at a little district school in Lenwick. Even though qualified teachers are as rare as hen's teeth nowadays, I am pretty confident I was graded an 'F'."

"Surely, they were just being... methodical?"

She shrugged. "I hope so. They said that they will confirm their decision next week. It is up to God now."

* * *

9.

"I'm sorry what?" Faith stood to her feet in a second. Any relief she felt when Mrs Martin came in person to meet with her, evaporated.

Gabe came and stood beside Faith and put a restraining hand on her shoulder. "Mrs Martin, there must be some mistake," he said. "There is no one more qualified for that position than Faith. She is educated. She has teaching qualifications. She has experience. She grew up in Lenwick. She understands the locals. She works well with children of all ages. These were all your own observations. Are you sure they are not going to consider her for this position?"

She sighed. "No. No, I am certain there is no mistake. Mind you it was not my choice. Given I only have an advisory role on the committee, and not a voting one, there is little more that I can do."

"Can you tell me who was appointed then?"

Mrs Martin squirmed awkwardly. "Miss Mirabella Rossi. She starts Monday."

Faith stared at Mrs Martin's face to see if she was joking. But she stood there, as serious as a judge handing down a sentence.

Gabe frowned. "But she has never shown any interested in being a teacher. Does she even have her graduating certificate?"

"She has a diploma... in.... Anyway, they feel her international cultural experience, and practical edge, offers our students opportunities that added weight to her application. She also speaks a second language... and you know that many of the local families speak Italian."

"What practical edge does have?" Mirabella didn't do anything practical when she had come to visit.

"Well... she has useful skills, like... cooking... that will enhance the student's learning experience."

Faith broke the silence by laughing. "Oh my! The boys are going to love this!"

"Miss Galloway!"

"Excuse my mirth, Mrs Martin. I wish your students all the best with their new... teacher." She gagged on the title and coughed ungainly as she opened the door.

Mrs Martin nodded and left, and Gabe turned to Faith with a raised brow. "Care to explain that?"

"I wish I could. I didn't appoint her."

"You were shooting the messenger. This was not Mrs Martin's doing. She was supportive of your application."

"Oh, come on! You cannot think that the improvement in my brothers' education, which was her defining argument, will be addressed by Mirabella? They either will be stunned into silence by her glorious beauty, or be scheming with even greater creativity, on how to get her to show more of her cleavage. Either way, their education is doomed. I know them." She took a shuddering breath.

"Faith?"

"Huh... I..." She ran her hand over her forehead and turned away. "I... I don't know what to do now. I didn't see this happening. How could it be possible to fail an interview for a small country school? I was so certain, that even if the interview did not go well, that what I knew on the train would still prevail. But evidently not. It has been a waste of time coming back."

"Following what you know to be right is never a waste."

"But I can't follow through if the school committee appoints someone else. It is out of my hands."

"Which part?"

"Gabe, you can't seriously be suggesting I stay here for a whole year without a job?"

"It wasn't my suggestion that you help your family. You said that is what you heard on the train. You can still do that part. If your mother needs you... and your brothers and your sisters need you... and you are in a position to make a difference, why wouldn't you? That's all you were asked to do."

"I make a difference at my other school as well! I left everything! And now I have no job! How can I possibly explain this to Worsley?"

"I don't think it is that complicated. You explained it to me. I got it. And I am just a simple carpenter."

"You know what I mean..."

"Faith, you've started strong; don't start wavering now. If it was always simple and straightforward, there would be no need for courage in our faith."

She glared at him for a long while, but he would not falter. Eventually she rolled her eyes and sighed. "Gabe Trimboli, I hate it when you are right."

He shrugged and grinned and picked up one of his mother's biscotti sitting on the bench.

She pursed her lips as she watched him munching. "This does leave me with a very practical problem. I assumed I would have the teacher's accommodation. Now I have nowhere to stay."

"You have here. We talked about that."

"But I can't stay here. Two unmarried people under the same roof."

"You're still spoken for. If you cook, I will reduce the rent which might help if you don't have a job. You're safe with me. Sounds like a pretty good deal."

"Well, I know that. But everyone else may think..." She shrugged.

"You are worried that they'll think you can no longer resist your childhood crush... and my charms will overwhelm you?"

"Or it could be that *you* will be unable to hold your wild affection in check... crazed by the beauty of my intellect."

He shook his head. "Faith, I wonder if you even realise your brain is not your only good quality?"

"Well apparently, even my brain is not smart enough to secure a job in a small country school. Perhaps I should have put on a prettier dress for the interview and perched on the school desk like a parrot."

He grinned. "Perhaps. Come on. Let's get out of here. We'll go and see your mother."

* * *

After they helped with the chores, they saddled the horses and went for a ride out past the boundary, up into the hills behind the property. They sat for a while overlooking the valley, while the horses ate grass behind them. "Were you serious about letting me stay at your place?"

"Well, if Mirabella has the teacher's accommodation, it'll mean I will have my bed back at home. As far as I know, Mamma hasn't kicked me out. I can work on the house while you are at school. Oh... huh, I'm sorry..."

"Are you seriously going to rub this in my face? We're not nine years old any more Gabe."

"It was a slip. I just can't get it in my head that they turned you down. Or... you could think of it as a declaration of trust. I still I believe you will be

Lenwick's school teacher... and soon. I can't even imagine Mirabella teaching kids. I give her a week."

"Your mother is a big campaigner for the Mirabella cause, so perhaps her influence was the swinging vote. It is not exactly breaking news that your mother doesn't approve of me."

"Only as a prospective wife, and that is because she is wholeheartedly deceived. I'm confident that as a tenant, there are no objections."

"I disagree. Her disapproval is far more sweeping – friend, tenant, teacher. I acutely felt my lack of Italian-ness growing up. I really wanted to belong to your big, busy, blustery, beautiful family."

"Perhaps the grass is greener on the other side of the fence. I used to watch your dad doing odd jobs on the little house next door to Nonni's... often by himself. I remember thinking how wonderful it would be just to have the space to work without a running commentary from every cousin within a fifty-mile radius. I enjoyed helping your dad doing that maintenance. He never said much, but he encouraged me that regardless of the problem, even if we can't fix it to be like new, the goal was always to make it better. And look, here I am... doing just that."

"Huh. Who would have thought that there would be cross pollination between our two very, very different families?" said Faith twirling a stem of flowering grass in her fingers.

"Cross pollination. Aren't you the horticulturalist? Remember that school project we did, trying to replicate the famous Monk Mendel's genetic experiments with garden peas?"

"Mendel? You remember that? I remember Philip loved that project so much that he took over... and we got an A. He still emphatically believes the study of genetics will unlock the treatment of some diseases. You know, when Philip chose medicine, I thought it was a bit of a come-down. Always thought he could do better than being a country doctor. But it seems he is more interested in medical research, rather than clinical practice. Perhaps he'll discover new treatments to old problems, which will offer more than just dealing out doses of tonic like Old Doc Mortimer."

"Doc Mortimer, in his own quiet way, was a hero of the profession. I wonder if he is why Philip wanted to become a doctor."

"Philip told me there was a particularly defining moment when we had the chickenpox as kids. He was so little... probably only five or six. Daisy was just a baby, and he was absolutely distraught when she became sick. Ma'ma caught it as well, and then we both came down with it. Philip was so worried that the chooks would catch it and their feathers would fall out. It is called Chicken Pox after all. But the chooks were fine. Most kids wouldn't even notice things like that, but Philip wanted to know why. Preventing something like Chicken Pox is probably not even possible. But who knows... one day they might actually work that out."

"Hmm. If anyone could come up with something like that, then Philip would be that person. He's always been a thinker who couldn't colour within the lines."

"Perhaps you're right. Mrs James never scoffed at these types of ambitions. She encouraged them. She changed my life, the way she inspired each of us in different directions. That is why I wanted to become a teacher. I wanted to nurture such dreams in other children, like she had for me... in the direction that is right for them."

"Mrs James vigorously challenged me when I was considering the carpentry apprenticeship with Old Henrik. She believed because I had the capacity for law, that I had an obligation to do it. But I made my choice and ended up working with timber. I went with what was satisfactory for my family. Practical seems better to them." He grinned. "Perhaps that's where Mirabella gets her practical edge."

Faith shook her head with a grimace. It was still stinging her pride that she was passed over for someone like Mirabella. "Is it satisfactory for you though Gabe?" Faith looked out over the valley. Her father said this view always offered a different perspective.

"Sort of. I know my job does not define me. The more important quest for me, regardless of what I do, is how am I striving to be a better person. Besides, the whole idea of real estate means I can dabble in property transfers and do my own conveyancing. I've studied the Torren's title system, and the Lands Act. I enjoy that side to it."

"Well, I envy your calm disregard of Mrs James' career advice."

"Mrs James was a visionary, and she always pushed her students forward. Her insistence on pursuing further studies was part of her extraordinary skill to make the exceptional look usual."

"And yet exceptional does not pay bills without a job. Even with a qualification, an exemplary resume, and previous experience, not having a job is still unemployment. I am struggling to work out if I can stay here without the position. I'm not sure I can."

"You're a teacher, right?"

"Of course." Faith folded the stem of grass she was holding and flicked off the flower-head like a missile. It landed in Gabe's lap. She inspected another before she picked it.

"It is not the position that makes you a teacher. That's just one opportunity to express it. Teaching is in your heart Faith. You were doing that even when you were in Grade Five... helping the younger ones with their homework. You are a teacher Faith, not just an employee. So be the teacher that is in your heart... find a way to do that, and we'll work out the money someway. Besides, I'm still not convinced that Mirabella will stick it out. If you leave, you won't have the chance to step in when the Board realises they have passed over the better candidate."

"Ma'ma said the same thing. Do you think Mirabella applied to the school because you like teachers?"

"I don't like teachers. Where did you get that idea?"

"Oh, I'm sorry. I thought you liked me. I am a teacher."

"Faith. You have not been listening. This is exactly my point. I do like you. But not because you graduated or became a teacher. I liked you long before any of that was ever on the horizon. And I would like you anyway, even if... you were something else like... I don't know, like a garbage collector or a politician... and I happen to find both of those career paths extremely unattractive. You know you will always be part of my life." His gaze penetrated her heart.

"Gabe... what are you doing? I..."

"I'm just trying to help you see that your family needs you to stay... actually all those kids do, especially if Mirabella is going to be their teacher. Please stay... for the children."

"For them... or for you?"

"Me? I can read and write. I don't need you to be my tutor, Miss Galloway." But the look that they shared told her a different story.

"Gabe... don't. I'm engaged."

He shrugged. "A point on which you are constantly reminding me. If the very handsome Mr Jones is who you say he is... nothing I say will make a difference. And if you are finding it does, then I wonder what that is telling you?"

"Grief! When did you become Mr *I-know-you-better-than-yourself?* You don't know me! I've been away for years!"

He stood up and backed away. "Don't forget we've both been away. But perhaps you are right. You are changed. The Faith I knew would not hesitate to help her family... or her community, regardless of the cost."

"Except you came back and I didn't. I have left Gabe! Why is no one hearing me? This is not my home anymore!"

"Faith, your family is still your family. You don't get to pick and choose them. They need you. That was the whole point of what happened on the train. This is not about me."

"Exactly! Then don't try and make it that way."

"I never said..."

"You don't have to *say* it. You know what I mean Gabe."

"I hear you loud and clear. This is me listening to you. I promised your mother I would help fix the gate on the chicken coup this afternoon, so I'd had better get back." He picked up his things and mounted his horse and didn't wait for her to follow.

* * *

10.

"Boys... where are Daisy and Violet?" They sniggered and shrugged... so innocently. Faith shook her head sternly as she was rolling dollops of biscuit mixture into balls and placing them on a baking tray.

"We ain't done nothing," defended Joe too quickly. Jimmy jabbed him.

"I have something I want to tell you all. Go and get them. Whatever you have done, go and release them now, so I can tell you together."

"But how could you know that they are...." Jimmy jabbed his brother harder. "Ow!"

"Go and get them right now! These biscuits will be ready for afternoon tea very soon."

Jimmy stomped off, muttering that his big sister was not his mother, and a giant pain in the you-know-where. The injustice of her interference smarted all the more because they harmlessly wanted to have 'a bit of fun'.

Faith was sliding the trays of biscuits out of the oven when Jimmy and Joe came skedaddling through the house with Daisy and Violet in hot pursuit. The girls were boiling and bothered, screaming blood curdling cries intent on extracting vengeance over whatever nasty little plot their brothers had committed.

Faith dumped the trays, whistled through her teeth, and stood in the doorway blocking their chase. She grabbed the boys by the collar as they screeched to a holt and then she sternly pulled the girls away as they went in for blood. "Greif! You all smell like the incinerator." She directed them to sit at the table. She poured them a drink of lemon squash, mixed from the cordial syrup they had made from their lemon tree. "Now calm down and take a breath. All of you. I have something to tell you." She removed her apron and took a squig of the lemon cordial, pushing a plate of warm ANZAC biscuits towards them. It was meant to be a bribe that would soften what was coming. Jimmy and Joe pounced on the biscuits. Daisy and Violet resigned their quest of revenge for now – kicking the boys under the table as they adjusted their chairs and took a biscuit each.

Faith cleared her throat. "I'm moving back to Lenwick to help Ma'ma out. Just until I am married next year. So when school starts, I'm going to be helping you catch up on your schoolwork. It has fallen behind terribly."

"What do you know? You ain't our teacher," protested Jimmy.

"If you cannot speak correctly Jimmy, I hardly need Ma'ma to show me your report cards. You can all do better, and I am going to help."

"How? We already go to school," said Joe, sticking his tongue out at Violet.

"Yes, and if you cannot manage to learn at school then we will have extra tuition to catch up. I am going to be your tutor."

A chorus of objections erupted. "What? No!"

"That sounds like a city-thing. This ain't the city."

"But school already takes all day."

"This is so unfair!"

"It's not our fault that Grey-Kaye is blind and dumb!"

"And it ain't our fault neither that he is a grunter!"

Faith stood up and slapped the table with the palm of her hand. "Enough! I don't expect you to like it. But Ma'ma and I have talked about this... and this is how it is going to be. You will get two hours after school before you come home. You need to improve if you are going to even be able to read a book before you leave school."

There were more objections. Daisy spoke up. "I can read, so that means I can skip this."

"No, it does not. Ma'ma tells me your maths and science need particular attention. All of you have been on an extended holiday. Well, that is over now. We will start when school resumes." Faith could tell Jimmy and Joe were already scheming how they would cut the designated lessons. Images flashed through her mind of directing search parties into the night to find the truants. "Just one more thing," she said. "I am renting rooms in Nonni Trimboli's old house, so you will be going there after school. We will have some afternoon tea together... and then we will work."

"What? That's stupid. Why can't we do it at home?"

"Because home is home... not school. And if you get within an inch of our gate, you will disappear like vapor, and I won't be able to find you. I am serious. This is not a competition to see how much you can get away with, but how you can improve. You are all very clever, but you're not getting the results you are capable of."

"I ain't going to be a doctor like Philip, so why should I have to? Stupid idea."

"There seems to be a proliferation of stupidity being thrown around. Stupid is a matter of ignorance. And *that* is what we are going to address. Doctors are not the only people who are educated. Just because you choose a different job does not disqualify you from needing an adequate schooling. Shopkeepers need to calculate sums quickly in their heads. Engineers need to be able to plan projects and write reports. Farmers need to understand seed ratios for planting or feeding stock. When Gabe is making furniture, he needs to measure and design things. Miss Townsend does the same thing when dressmaking and ordering fabrics."

"I know plenty of adults who can't read and write. They do okay."

"And that may be no fault of their own. But their life would be easier if they could. If my brothers and sisters grow up illiterate... that will be on me. So it is not going to happen. Just letting you know."

When their mother appeared rocking little Edith-Rose, she looked at their surly faces. "Hmm, I take it Faith has told you about the plan to improve your grades? I don't want you fighting her on this. It is important, so we are going to do it. Understood?"

They groaned. The boys grabbed a fist full of biscuits and fled outside to capture the last shred of daylight before being called in for dinner. The girls disappeared in the opposite direction.

Faith sat down and reached for a lone broken biscuit on the tray. "Oh Ma'ma, it appears the picture I had in my head of imparting make-up lessons, with my brothers and sisters hanging on my every word, may not actually look how I imagined it. They are going to fight me all the way on this, aren't they?"

Salome smiled at her daughter. "Most likely. Are you sure you are up for it?"

"I have to be. I know Mr Kaye is an educated man, but he is odd and old fashioned. Mrs Martin was right about that. I hold little hope that between him and Miss Rossi, they could adequately achieve anything resembling an education." She stood up with a sigh. "Well, I'd better go and tell Gabe the news, and see if he is still willing to rent me his rooms. I'm guessing he's not going to be happy about it either. All I do, at the moment, is be the bearer of uncomfortable news."

"I thought you said Gabe encouraged you to stay and help."

"Oh Ma'ma. It's Gabe. He spins on a dime. We had a bit of a falling out. Again."

"Honey, do you think he still has feelings for you? You both seem to spark like crackers on Guy Fawkes Night."

"You might be right... but I can't think about it. I just can't. I am engaged."

"I don't know Worsley... but I know Gabe. And I am confused how someone who has been a steadfast friend your entire life, is now accused of being fickle and unreliable. Are you being fair, Faith?"

"Fair or otherwise, I am about to become his tenant... that is, if he will still let the rooms to me. I am not really sure how this is going to pan out."

"Just don't forget to be kind to old friends. How you treat others reflects who you are, regardless how long you have known them."

"Oh, I wish I had just said yes when Mrs Martin asked me about the job in the first place. That would have made this so much simpler. I would have a job and the accommodation that goes with it."

"Perhaps it might have been simpler to do it that way, but I am a firm believer that God is bigger than any of our doubts. God can still work this out for the best. Remember that... even when it seems to be all falling apart. Our responsibility is to stay sweet... and keep going."

* * *

She knocked at the door and called out. "It's Faith." She wondered if he would blockade the door and tell her to leave, just as she had heard him firmly refuse entry to Mirabella.

There was a pause, and he opened the door and stepped aside silently. Part of her was still surprised every time Gabe didn't impose an extended period of punishment after their arguments. "Thank you for letting me in."

"Why wouldn't I?"

"I don't know... we had a disagreement before. Worsley would make me sweat it out a bit." A lot.

"Well, I am not him. What did you want?"

"I wanted to see if you are still willing to let a room to me. I've told the kids that I will be doing tutoring after school. An idea which they hate of course... but if I cannot be their schoolteacher during the day, then there is really no other way they will get the help they need. I also told them I would do it here, and not at home. I am hoping that might reduce the likelihood of them deserting. I could see Jimmy calculating his escape even while I was talking to them."

"Hmm. So you want a room for tutoring as well. Two rooms."

"I'll pay you Gabe. Somehow. Probably not much... but I'll try. I am hoping there may be other students who want tutoring. I would charge them something."

"So how is this going to work... if we are both working in the same house?"

"Like it does now I guess."

"But you told me this is a concern for you. Even if I sleep at home, I still need to work on the house."

"Well, I was thinking I would go out and help Ma'ma in the mornings... chores and the like... washing, getting dinner prepared... that sort of thing... and then I'll come in after lunch to do marking and prep. That will give you the morning to work on the house, and then there might be quieter things you could do while I have students here. I'll be gone in the morning and there will be students around in the afternoon."

"Are you satisfied that we will be suitably supervised, and your honour will be held accountable?"

"I thought it might reassure your mother. She won't like me being here."

"Hmm. Maybe. On a brighter note, if you are here tutoring, then that would mean I could not have visitors drop in after school... namely Mirabella. Your students should not be distracted. I think this arrangement has a blissful edge of convenience for me."

"I could still cook your meals like you suggested, and maybe do other things for you as well. I'll take you up on your offer to reduce the rent if I take on chores... like washing, or working Nonni's vege garden, or looking after the chooks... that sort of thing."

He grinned. "Sounds like you are really moving in to take over my household for twelve months. I might get used to the domestic ease of this arrangement and want to keep you."

"I am not marrying you Gabe. It is payment-in-kind... for rent. Nothing more."

"So you keep reminding me. Still sounds like a legally binding contract. I'll write it up."

"Seriously. You want me to sign it?"

He shrugged. "Call it, the frustrated Lawyer in me wanting to get out of the sandpit and climb a tree."

"Unbelievable. It is a shame you know how to read, or I could tutor you as well. Very well. I'll start dinner."

* * *

I I.

Gabe arrived early in the morning and was soon hammering and making a racket. Faith emerged from her room bleary eyed. "What's going on?"

"Working. Need to get a jump on the day," he said cheerily.

She went over and took the kettle off the stove that was already starting to whistle. "How is it possible that you can be so jovial this early in the morning?"

"Well, you promised me breakfast, so I didn't want you to miss your chance to pay rent before you go out to your Mamma's place."

She groaned and rubbed her eyes and stretched. "So the arrangement begins. Breakfast time."

"This is a tenanted arrangement after all – rent is required," he said tackling the next plank. He turned away with a grin as he levered and hammered some more timber off the wall, stacking the planks in a pile, as she started to cook.

Faith poured a couple of cups of coffee and put them on the table. Faith served his plate, placed his breakfast in front of him and sat down opposite.

He thanked her and said grace. "You're not eating?"

"It's too early. I've just woken up, and suddenly I'm in the middle of a reconstruction. My head is realigning that's all." She stared at the wall that was coming down. "I thought you said that the work you are doing is cosmetic. This looks structural," she said with a frown.

"Hmm. Was looking over the main living area at your Mamma's place. I like how it provides space for family just being family. This wall is not loadbearing and doesn't serve any purpose other than to create the hallway. I've decided to take it out to open the space up a bit. Which room did you want to use for your classroom? I'll paint it before you move your things in. School starts soon, and I figured you'd want it ready by then. That timeline is another reason I've started early."

She blinked. And then blinked again. She went to say something, and then stopped, drinking her coffee with a shake of her head.

"What?" He picked up his mug and drank his coffee.

"Nothing. This is unexpected that's all!" She looked away frowning. "Are you really giving me a choice of which room I take for tutoring? I just assumed it would be the little room, next to my bedroom. I thought that if I swapped my bed into the smaller one, I would have more space for the kids to sit at a table."

"That room is like a closet. Why don't you take the front room...it is larger and closer to the front door?"

"Are you sure?"

"That would be the practical choice, especially if other children are coming and going. I'm being a considerate landlord here." He paused. "I also had another idea. This timber I'm taking down... I'm going to use it to make desks and forms for the kids."

"Gabe!"

"What? They are going to need something to sit on. And I have to do something with the timber."

"No... it's just. You are..." She rubbed her forehead. His big-hearted generosity was just like his grandmother. "You do realise that these twelve months of tutoring is my assignment. You don't have to do this."

"Doesn't mean I can't help. You're helping your family. And I can help you. That's fair."

"But I am not your family Gabe."

"Oh, I would say you are definitely family to me Faith. You always have been... well... at least since you danced with me that night at your parent's wedding here in the backyard. We have history in this house that goes a long way back."

"You are doing it again..."

"No, I'm not. I understand you are going to marry your David. You do what you need to do in that department. I won't interfere. But that doesn't mean I'm going to just abandon you to the antics of your brothers in the meantime. You didn't hesitate to help me in the trenches with Mirabella. I can't help with the lessons, but I can do background stuff. I'm here to do that. Why can't I help you?"

"It doesn't seem right."

"Mirabella took your job. That doesn't seem right either. There is a lot of things around that aren't right. We just do what we can to help each other work through them. It is just like your dad used to say... even if it is not perfectly right, we do what we can to make it less wrong. Most things, I've discovered, have scratches across the surface."

She pushed her mug aside and stood up. "More toast?" He nodded. She cooked herself a piece on the stovetop as well. When she sat down, she looked uncertain. "Well...since I'm here, would it be okay if I help you paint the tutoring room?"

"Of course. I'm just here to help Faith, not take over."

"But this is your home. You will want it a particular way."

"And for the next year... it is yours as well. I'll be taking in some furniture jobs and since Henrick's Workshop is not available anymore I'm setting up a workshop downstairs. See, I have things I have to adjust from the picture in my head as well. I'll still give Papa a couple of days here and there. But the first thing is fixing up the front room so you can start your tutoring." He pulled a sheet of paper from his pocket and pushed it over towards her. He had mapped out a position of four student desks and chairs. A blackboard. A teacher's table and chair. A bookcase. "We'll start with four desks. I'll make more so they're ready when other students start."

"What's this going to cost?"

"What are you talking about?"

"Furniture costs money... which I don't have."

He shrugged. "I have the timber, and I'm making the desks for the kids. I'm not going to charge them. Besides, it'll be a chance to showcase what I can do. Another thing, what colour do you like?"

"Colour?"

"Paint. For the walls."

"I prefer plain, light, neutral." Well actually, Worsley liked neutral.

He nodded dubiously. "I bet you were thinking I intend to slather the entire house in Tuscan terracotta," he said with a grin.

Faith stared at him for a moment, and then went over to the bench and picked up one of the loose patterned ceramic tiles from the kitchen bench. She put it on the table. "These colours are everything that reminded Nonni of Italy. So how would you feel if we used this theme. Neutral with these old-world accents. Tuscan charm, but with a modern touch."

"The tutoring room... or the entire house?"

"Either."

"I keep reminding you that Italian is not marketable or profitable. Otherwise, why would Lenwick have the 'White Pub' and 'The Other Pub'. I definitely belong to the 'Other' one."

"There are plenty of people in this area who would appreciate this style: regardless of their cultural mix. That's working *to* your market."

"Does it appeal to you?"

"Of course it does. Nonni converted me to this palate a long time ago. I tried for years to convince Ma'ma to paint our loungeroom deep red. She refused of course. And her disinclination to cooperate always left me with a sense of frustration. I might finally get it out of my system."

"You've just gone from bland to bright in the space of a minute. What happened to 'plain, light, and neutral'."

"Neutral is less distracting for the students. Oh, all right, I confess... I enjoyed Nonni's splash of colour. It always seemed bright, and fun, and cheerful compared to our dull little house next door. It suited her, and it suits this house."

"You know this officially makes you my decorator – for the whole house. Although I will reserve the right-of-veto if I don't like it. I have to live with this, long after you go back to your city Mrs Jones."

She grinned. "Fair enough. This time next year I will definitely be Mrs Jones."

* * *

12

The walls of the front room were scrubbed. The old paint was tired and dull, and well and truly overdue for a freshen-up. They spread out large drop-sheets over the floor to protect the polished timber and went to work. Gabe came home with paint – light and neutral. Faith started in the corner painting the tongue-in-groove joins, while Gabe followed behind her with a broader brush. They alternated using the ladder. Their easy banter was good natured. One wall.

"That didn't take long! We make quite a team," said Faith as they took a break before tackling the next section.

"So how did you want to bring in the colour? Accents on the sills and architraves?" asked Gabe with a nod as he handed her a cup of coffee.

Faith retrieved a loose tile from Nonni's bench, and she pointed to the detail of a pattern around the centre motif. "This dark red is the exact colour of the ribbon I chose for the very first dress Dad had Miss Townsend make for me."

"I remember that dress. That was the one you wore to the wedding... when we had our first dance."

She shook her head and stepped back. "I'm surprised you remember what I was wearing..."

He grinned and shrugged. "What can I say – you made an impression Miss Galloway."

She pointed to the tile. "Do you think this is too bold for a tutoring room?"

"I have Italian blood... I am comfortable with bold. The question is whether you think your students will find it distracting. It's not neutral."

"Hmm, well, I also don't want them going to sleep either. Engaging and stimulating are also factors to consider."

He raised his brow in approval. "I could do up a couple of poster frames. Same colour."

"More accents. Nice. The frames would be a tidy solution for maps, or posters of multiplication tables. That is a great idea."

"Well Miss Galloway. It seems you are going to have your classroom, even without the job at the school."

"You know, getting in and doing this has taken the sting out of the committee's rejection a bit. Thank you."

"Another coffee, and then back to work. We'll do a final coat and I'll order the pigments to mix this rustic red."

* * *

Faith finished painting the windowsill and poster frames, using the red Gabe had blended to match the tile. She had all but finished the last of the colour in her little pot. It was just perfect. She put down her tin and looked at Gabe in his overalls. There were streaks of paint through his dark hair. She remembered Flynn, her stepfather, having that same look about him when Ma'ma first started looking after Daisy. Paint splatter over his clothes. Perhaps fixing things up was what Lenwick men did. She didn't say anything for a long time. Gabe went to load his brush again. He must have sensed her looking at him because he paused and looked up. He caught her gaze and their eyes connected. He didn't say anything, and he didn't move, suspended over his paint tin.

After a long silence, Faith swallowed. "Why don't we work? We should. It makes sense that we should."

Gabe put down his brush and rocked back on his haunches and stayed there. He waited. "I thought we did. This is us working Faith. Rather well, I thought."

"No. I mean, why didn't we fall madly in love and marry as childhood sweethearts? It's a common enough story around here. Why not us?"

How often had he wanted an answer to that same question? Who said he didn't – the first part anyway. He pulled over a paint tin and sat on it. "Why do you think that is?"

"I think... I think I wouldn't let it."

"What do you mean?"

"I mean..." She swallowed hard and adjusted the shoulder straps on her overalls. This was a confession she had never spoken out before. Her heart raced and felt like it would stop any moment from the shame of it. "I mean... I was scared. I thought about what you said the other day, about trying to balance everyone's expectations. All those big voices in my life, Ma'ma and Dad. Mrs James and Nonni. Even you. The consistent theme was not to stay; to go and study and be great. But great was never here in Lenwick. It was always somewhere else."

"Couldn't great be here too?"

"That's just it. Every single one of these people countered their own argument just by being themselves! Each one of them was great. Nonni was great. Dad. Mrs James... she was the greatest teacher. Ma'ma... They are all people who are great. And they did it here! Why was I not allowed to be great here? I feel like they were pushing me away because I was not enough to stay. That I had to go somewhere else, to somehow measure up."

"Faith, wow. I had no idea you thought that. You have always been enough. But I was afraid that Lenwick might not be big enough for you."

"Why didn't you tell me that?"

"I thought you would resent Lenwick's smallness, and then resent me if I tried to keep you here."

"You wanted me to stay? I didn't know that."

"Of course. I still do. But I can't tell you that."

"Why not?"

"Because it has to be your choice to be here Faith. My choice is this: to still be around until I find out what you are going to choose. Until I know for sure that Lenwick is not an option for you, I'm here. If you decide, definitely, finally, that I am not part of your future, then I will move on. But I cannot... I won't move... not until I know that it's final."

She dropped her brush into a bucket of water and came over to him. "I wish you had said that before," she said looking down at him sitting on the paint tin.

"I'll say this," he said quietly, standing up, looking into her face, eye to eye. "I would like to kiss you again. And as soon as you take that ring off your finger, that will be one of the first things I will do."

She stepped away and fled, knocking her near empty paint pot as she left. He heard her drive away shortly after, the old jalopy backfiring as she left. He sat down and looked at the toppled paint tin in a detached sort of way. It felt surreal almost, that he had declared those things. He closed his eyes and ran his hand across his forehead, the paint on his finger smearing into his hairline. He had probably said too much. Still, if he knew Faith, and he did, she would be back, and there would be another honest, if uncomfortable, exchange.

A vehicle drove up and there was a knock on the door. Bingo. Right on cue.

He opened the door and there stood a tall man. Gabe looked him over. Dark hair. Curly. Chiselled features. Fashionable Homburg hat. Smart suit. "Hmm. You must be David."

"Who? No, you are mistaken. My name is Worsley. Worsley..."

"Jones," they said in unison.

"Oh. Then you know of me. I was looking for my fiancé. Faith Galloway? I was told she is renting here." He looked dubiously past him into the house, unconvinced as to the reliability of such a report.

"She just left."

"Do you know where she went? Where would I find her?"

"Huh. She didn't say."

"Oh. Well, I presume she will come back. I will wait here. And you are?" He looked him over with a dismissive glance; his splattered worker's overalls, and the paint smears in his hair said all he really needed to know.

"The landlord. Fixing up the place."

"Hmm."

"And I'm not comfortable inviting a stranger into my tenant's house."

"But I told you: we are engaged."

"You're not engaged to me. I don't know you. You need to go."

Worsley frowned. And even with his disgruntled bearing, Gabe felt compelled to acknowledge, as far as the David precedent went – of 'ruddy and handsome' appearance, Jones really did meet the brief. Gabe turned away and went to close the door. Jones stuck his boot into the gap.

Gabe raised his brow. "Really? Are you forcing your way into the house? My guess is that charges of breaking and entering, would not sit comfortably on your smart city collar. She's not here, and it is not my job to babysit Miss Galloway's visitors."

"Well, you're an unpleasant sort of chap, aren't you?"

Chap? Even that word, companiable when others said it, sounded obnoxious on his lips. "As I said, it is also not my job to amuse you with pleasantries. Excuse me, I have work to do."

Jones withdrew his boot, and Gabe firmly closed the door on him. He shook his head, rubbed his temple as he looked around the tutoring room, at the paint pots, drop-sheets and ladder. This morning they had worked together so agreeably. He sighed and went back to painting.

* * *

"So... David was here."

Faith's fork stayed suspended in the air as she stared at him in shock. "David? As in Worsley? He's here? In Lenwick? Why didn't you say something before? Where is he now?"

He shrugged. "Dunno. You know – he looks continental. Tall, dark. You really do have a thing for Italians."

"I told you he was good-looking. Didn't you believe me?"

"I believe that..." He stopped himself and tried to think of something that would not sound twisted and jealous. He had nothing. He resented that Jones was as handsome as Mirabella was beautiful. He had hoped that when David spoke, his voice would sound squeaky and thin. That would be fitting. But it resonated with a rich timbre. Grief. That was not fair either.

"Did he say where he was staying?"

"He did not."

"Or when he would be back?"

"Nope."

"You are not being very helpful."

"Nice of you to notice."

"I notice you are jealous."

"Can't deny it."

"Gabe, this is ridiculous. You have had a lifetime to declare yourself. And you only get around to it, when I have found someone who would step up for me. This is not my fault. I am engaged!"

"That sounds like an evasive manoeuvre to me. You have always known what I think. Our friendship spans our entire lives. But I was evidently right: Lenwick is too small and not sophisticated enough for the great Faith Galloway."

"Don't you dare! That is not fair!"

"I do dare... because what is not fair is that I am waiting around on your good will and pleasure. Well, roll on this year, because I am getting tired of not knowing! Ever since you have come back, the one consistent message I get is that you are not sure. You try to convince yourself you are, but nothing you have said sounds certain to me. You have this idea in your head of who you are... but when we get in and start cleaning and painting, suddenly you are you again. Faith, do you really want to say goodbye to that person completely? Because if you marry *that* David... you will never find her again. That is one thing I am certain of."

"You don't know that Gabe Trimboli. You know nothing!"

"I do. You don't even know where to find him. And yet you always seem to know where I am."

"That's because Lenwick has three streets and four houses! And you never go anywhere! That's hardly a challenge."

"And yet you lost your David... and he couldn't find you either."

"Oh! You are infuriating!"

"Actually, I think more accurately, I am just honest. And you are annoyed because I keep calling you out on this ideal picture in your head. Life has scratches Faith. What happens when you wake up and find David has wrinkles? The only way that won't happen is if he is carved out of marble. But then again, looking at him... he just might be."

"Oh!" She slammed down her fork and stormed outside.

* * *

13.

Faith's mother served the plates and was about to sit down at the table, when little Edith-Rose started to cry. She apologised and went to attend to her. Faith directed her brothers and sisters to say grace and they began to eat. She cut up Gus's food and helped him with his dinner. Violet kicked Jimmy under the table when he started to flick peas into Daisy's drink, who was reading a book, hidden in her lap under the tablecloth.

Worsley cleared his throat and raised his brow. This was a side of Faith's life that he had never witnessed before. "Well, it is a pleasure to meet you all," he said with a winning smile.

Joe looked at him. "You gunna take us riding like Gabe does?"

"I think an outing like that would be quite agreeable." He glanced at Faith who frowned and shook her head cautiously. "I can ride. It won't be a problem," he insisted.

"I think *that* is something to discuss with Ma'ma. Boys, eat your dinner, rather than using it as projectiles. Daisy... reading at the table is poor manners. Put the book away." Daisy huffed and rolled her eyes... and kept reading. "Violet, are you going to eat anything? Are you feeling okay?"

Violet shook her head. Joe poked his tongue out at her, and she barely blinked. "Stupid," she said back at him.

Jimmy took advantage of the distraction to plant some bugs in Worsley's mashed potato. And he sniggered as Worsley gagged on a mouthful of potato, laced with critters. Worsley hurriedly pushed his back chair and went outside. They could hear him retching over the rail. Worsley's hope had been that if he ate quickly, the cruelty of this family meal would be over sooner. He returned after a while and stoically sat back down to a stony silence. He suspiciously pushed his food around the plate with the fork. An expression of realisation dawned on his face as he immediately stood up again. A puddle of gravy was now smeared all over the seat of his pants.

Jimmy was sent to his room. Faith found a pair of her dad's work trousers that had not been discarded. He emerged from the room with mortification written all over his face. The pants were shabby and far too short for Worsley's tall legs. She watched him resume his seat, held captive, bracing himself to endure the next phase of torture to be inflicted. Faith had heard reports about the Japanese POW camps during the war, and the ruthless treatment of prisoners held there. Her father had been one of those prisoners. And he didn't survive. Yet here her family was being no less shocking.

When dinner was over, she brought Worsley a cup of tea as they settled on the lounge. He looked at the cup warily. She shook her head. "I made it myself. It is safe."

"I doubt that is any guarantee, unless your family is either locked up or unconscious."

She sat down beside him. "Thank you for trying. I know they are difficult."

"Difficult? You can't be related to these people Faith! You are intelligent and sophisticated. I feel like I have been dropped behind enemy lines in hostile territory. Or dumped in a swamp full of monsters. It challenges the idea that bunyips are mythical. No wonder you left!"

"That's a little harsh. This is my family."

"Exactly my point. How is it possible that you grew up here?"

"It is possible, and this is exactly why my mother needs help. It is too much for her."

"So you are completely serious? You are going to stay... without a job? You can't stay for a whole year. That is downright preposterous!"

"I can. And I will."

"Well, I think it would have been appropriate to discuss this with me before making such a radical decision."

"Why? So you could talk me out of it?"

He stared at her with a frown, shocked that she was being so candid. He spoke low, just above a whisper. "Faith, did you fall into that swamp and turn *bunyip* as soon as you arrived here? You need to consider your position and your reputation. This impacts us both!" His voice grated like fingers scratching down a chalkboard. Faith blinked. How was that possible? Was he actually related to Mirabella?

"There is nothing wrong with my reputation, and I consider my position is to help my family. How can you not support such a basic family ethic?"

"I support you. Of course I do. You are my fiancé. I'm not sure about this though. It is messy and uncouth. Your mother needs to take control of the situation."

"Perhaps she needs support!" Faith stood up furious. "We are going. Now!" She went into the other room, and quickly said goodbye to her mother, and grabbed her coat. She shook her head. This is exactly why she didn't say anything to him before she came back. She knew it would be a battle. But this time there would be no retreat. No white flag. No armistice achieved by only accepting his terms.

Predictably on the drive back to Nonni's house, Worsley went quiet. But instead of starting her usual ritual of cajoling him to relent and talk, Faith took full advantage of the fact he had hunkered down silently in his trenches. "Worsley, whether you like it or not my family is not part of any negotiation here. I'm not excusing their behaviour, but no one gets to choose their family. Just as you don't get to choose yours." It felt like the voice of Gabe was echoing around in her head. But she didn't pause. "It is obvious that Ma'ma needs me here for a time. It is very reasonable that I stay under these circumstances. This is something you will have to accept."

He interjected, unable to stay quiet any longer. "That's ridiculous. I am not marrying your family Faith! I'm engaged to *you*. And besides, my family never behaves like that!"

Faith smiled into the shadows as they turned into the street. He had not stayed aloof. Predictable-Worsley just broke ranks. That was unexpected. "Of course, your family doesn't look like this. You are an only child. But I have never judged you, even though you don't know how to share, or have fun."

"Fun? That's the most absurd thing I have ever heard. There is nothing fun about marauding around like a barbarian mob! You can't judge my family because there is nothing wrong with them to start with." He pulled the car to a stop outside Nonni's house and turned to her. "Faith what has got into you? You are behaving quite irrationally."

"Hang on, this is *my* barbarian mob, my tribe, my clan... and I happen to love them! Perhaps you are getting to see who I have always been."

"Again... ridiculous! You haven't always been like this. It is like I am meeting an entirely different person."

Faith pushed out her hand. "Then let me introduce myself. My name is Faith Lilly Galloway. Faith – my ongoing belief in God. Lilly – my mother's quirky fascination for flower names... which happens to mean peace, purity and faith. I am pleased to meet you Mr Jones."

He turned away. "That is not even funny." His eyes settled on the bare bulb alight under the house, where Gabe had set up his workshop. "Why is the landlord working under your house?"

"He has a workshop there. He is a carpenter and taking in some extra jobs. He is making furniture... including some desks for the tutoring room."

"He should reduce the rent if he continues to use the premises for income purposes. Typical. Ethnics always have a finger in some dodgy pie. You should be careful. Who knows what else he is selling from there?"

Faith scoffed. How could he charge less than nothing? Worsley was so quick to judge something he knew nothing about! "He is not part of the Italian Mafia. This is Lenwick! Gabe is the least dodgy person I know."

"Why didn't you just apply for the schoolteacher's job? Then you wouldn't have to go to all the bother trying to set up a tutoring service."

"That's a great idea Worsley. Perhaps you could speak to the school committee on my behalf." She turned away and rolled her eyes, as she opened the door. More informed ignorance.

"Wait," he said. She paused and turned back with a raised brow. "Aren't you going to kiss me good night? When will I see you tomorrow?" he asked impatiently.

"I will be going out to help Ma'ma in the morning. You can meet me out there. Goodnight Ga... Worsley. Goodnight." She swallowed hard, and she walked up the stairs and opened the door. Nonni's lamp sitting on the table near the entry was the only light on. She put down her things and sat in the shadows for a long time. She and Worsley had just had their first significant fight. It was strange and exhilarating and disturbing. How could she be marrying a man she never had to make up with? She realised they never fought simply because she never resisted any of his inflexible opinions. Her mother had always said she was a peacemaker by nature. But this, Faith realised, this was not peace. This was war pushed underground. He always had a perspective, and a solution, or a good idea, and she always accepted them. How would this work if she chose to be completely honest about the imperfections in their life? Her opinions mattered too. Perhaps Gabe was right. Perhaps a real David would have wrinkles. She was curious to discover how they might iron out these relationship wrinkles in their life together.

She made a couple of cups of coffee and took them downstairs to where Gabe was working. He didn't look up but stayed focused on joining some of the boards together. She put his cup down on the bench and perched on a box beside him.

"So how did that go, meeting the family?" he asked, lining up some timber.

"Terrible. He hates my family."

Gabe did glance up then and grinned as he finished clamping the wood on his bench. "That's good news," he said without apology. He picked up his cup and took a drink of his coffee.

"No, it's not. It's appalling! He called our living-room a Bunyip Swamp."

He laughed. "And he said I was 'an unpleasant sort of chap'. That is the pot calling the kettle black, if ever I heard it."

Faith looked at the progress on the desks and offered to hold some of the timber for him as he nailed. They worked together, comfortably for a while. "You should be able to start painting this desk tomorrow."

"Oh. We are painting the desks?"

"Yes. Paint. It's too much to try and strip the boards all back to timber. Besides, Tuscan highlights remember. What colour do you want?"

She picked up a kitchen tile that was on the workbench and turned it around in the light like she was examining a gemstone. "Umm. Okay. Here's an idea. A different colour for each of the desks. I want all the tile colours: Rustic-red, Marzipan-cream, Teal-green, Tuscan-terracotta, and Nautical-blue."

He grinned. "You have even named your tones. Very Mediterranean. I'll make an Italian out of you yet."

"These tiles... are you replacing the kitchen ones?"

"Will probably have to. I don't think I can match them, and there are quite a few that are broken and chipped."

"What if we used them as a featured insert for something... like a wooden planter?"

"I like that. You are quite good at this."

"Well thank you," she said with a smile. "And don't throw out any of the chipped tiles... I think we could use them to mosaic some other ideas."

"Well, Miss Galloway, you are showing quite a creative streak. And here I was thinking 'plain, light, and neutral' meant that we wouldn't get to play with any creative options at all."

She looked at him curiously. "And yet I get the feeling you would have done it all plain and neutral any way. This is your house Gabe. You can paint it however you want."

"I know. I just want to do it this way. With you."

"Well, I'm exhausted, so I'm off to bed. I will see you in the morning."

"I've had plenty of coffee, so I'm going to work here for a while. At least finish this bit. Good night."

Faith climbed into bed and smiled as she heard the muted sounds of Gabe working downstairs. It was comforting to know he was there... building. She dozed off and slept soundly.

* * *

"Worsley, you did what?"

"I told you. I had a meeting with the Chairman of the school committee. I spoke to him about appointing you to the schoolteacher's position. You have every credential. It was just about presenting your case confidently."

"No! You didn't!"

"You asked me to. I said I would, and I did."

She looked at him sideways. How could he take her sarcasm so literally? "And what did he say?"

"Well, he said I made some good points, and he would take it to the committee. You will start at the beginning of the school year."

"He said that?"

"Well, no. But..."

"Ahh... he is *'taking it under advisement'*." She groaned. "Worsley, saying that is Lenwick-speak for *'mind your own business'*. I will never be considered for the role now. Period. You should have left it alone." She never anticipated that having an education would be such a disadvantage. She knew rural townsfolk were suspicious of book-learning, perhaps because it was so inaccessible to most of them. Was it fear? Was it jealousy? They said it made people out of touch with the practical matters of real life. It dawned on her that Worsley held it with equal suspicion.

He stood tall and tilted his chin. "You were not there, and you cannot presume to know how that conversation went. I will guarantee that I convinced him of your suitability for the position. I expect you will hear something by the end of the week. It was simply a matter of putting a strong foot forward."

"Pretty sure I know what I am talking about," she said with a frown.

He patted her hand, and she pulled away. "We will see. We will see," he said. "I know what I know... and I know how to read people. That is why I am good at my job."

"Hmm. I am going to suggest you might be adept at reading a certain type of situation but that does not make you an authority on everything and everyone." She noticed that he was missing reading her completely. "Why didn't you talk to me about this? I have ..."

"Really? You are lecturing me on communication? You came here without talking to me at all. I get a short letter, without any reassurance that you appreciate how uncomfortable this whole debacle is. What does that say about our relationship Faith? I am not one of your school-yard pupils. We are to be married. You will not even work after this year anyway, so I don't know why you are making all this fuss about tutoring third-graders out in the boondocks as if it is some high-powered career move."

"What are you talking about?"

"I'm talking about the demographic here... it is not exactly a..."

"No. About not working..."

"Well of course when we are married, you will not need to work anymore. We are engaged, remember? Why is it that you are constantly overlooking this? Did you fall and hit your head when you stepped off the train? Because it appears you have forgotten a whole lot of things since you have come back to Lenwick. What has got into you? We will be married, and married women don't work."

"I would disagree. Married women work very hard. They might not get paid or receive any recognition for it. You sound like those who think the pinnacle of a woman's achievement is emptying night-waste from under the bed! I thought you supported me in pursuing these ideals."

"As an educated young woman your ambitions have been quite flattering and reasonable. But once you are married, you know that is entirely different."

"Pretty sure I didn't know that. How is it different? I am still the same person and I hold the same views."

"No, what is different is that you and I will be married. That is a significant change. The war is over. It is right that life goes back to normal. This is exactly what we were fighting for. After everything we have been through, it is appropriate you stay to look after our home. I am here to provide for you. We don't need the extra income."

"This is not about the money! You cannot expect that I give up everything I have worked for, just because you want a housekeeper!"

"Housekeeper? Really? Is this how you see our marriage?"

"It is evident that's how you see it! I have worked hard to accomplish my goals. I am the same person," she repeated.

"I would argue that you are not the same person I met at all. I feel you have duped me, Faith. Entrapped me in an engagement just because you wanted a professional husband."

"Is that right? Entrapped? You say my take on our relationship is harsh, yet your own assessment is equally damning. Do you have any confidence in me at all?"

"Right now, you are right: my confidence is pretty shot." She shook her head in disbelief, as he continued very firmly. "I think we need to take a break so you can decide what you want, because all of this... this is not what I want. Not at all."

"Take a break? What are you saying?"

"I'm saying that this is becoming quite unmanageable. If you decide to stay here in Lenwick for a whole year, our engagement will not survive."

"We survived the entire war! How can we not survive peacetime?"

"Exactly. I waited at your insistence. This extended separation is not appropriate. I'm done waiting. I wonder if you really want to marry me at all. It would be ludicrous to consider marriage under these circumstances."

"What is ludicrous is that first you say I've entrapped you, and then you follow that up by saying I am avoiding marrying you. Make up your mind Worsley!"

"Okay. Done. My mind is made."

"No! We don't have to split like this. It is just one year! Then I am back."

"No, it is not just one year. It is a divide too wide for us to cross. It is your choice Faith. I am leaving tomorrow. You should come with me. If you do, it is entirely possible we could fix this mess. But I am going to be definite about one thing. We cannot be married out here. It needs to be in town with our family and friends, just like we wanted in the first place."

Faith noticed his imperial sweeping use of the word "*we*" with a sigh. Her family didn't count. She didn't count. "So let me understand. If I get on the train tomorrow... you will concede to marry me. Otherwise, our relationship is over?"

"Now who is harshly manipulating what is said? What I am saying is that this... this is too much. I fell in love with the Faith who is from town... not this Lenwick-Farm-Faith whom I don't even recognise. I should have seen this coming when you insisted on being married out here in the boondocks."

She stared at him. She could hardly hear what he said after that. It sounded like more of the same. On and on. Worsley didn't like scratches either. But this wasn't just a little mark on the surface; this was covered in deep gouges. She knew that it wasn't perfect. Still, it was her family, and her life, and her mess. She remembered that the real David in the Bible had lived in caves for many years, long before he was ever a king. He led a band of displaced, unpolished, rough discontents. That was a scratched-up mess as one could get. Yet out of that mess came a great King of Israel. It occurred to her then, that perhaps Worsley was like King Saul... tall, good looking, competent, but he didn't have to do it rough like the David who lived in caves. Saul didn't have to hone or protect his character because no one ever challenged his scratches. He never lived with the mess. The king that Saul became, was like the vain Greek god Narcissus. It was a moment of revelation for her. She didn't want to marry Narcissus, no matter how good looking he was.

"Well, I guess I will see you in the morning at the train station," she finally said.

"There. That is better. I knew I could make you see reason."

"Good night, Worsley."

* * *

Faith did not sleep. She cried into her pillow. The shame and disappointment were burning holes in her chest. She felt like that fancy Swiss cheese Worsley's parents had a fondness for. Or like someone had taken a spoon handle and poked holes in her, not unlike those cakes her mother would make for their birthdays when they were young. But the difference was that her mother would fill those holes with a lovely, sweet, stewed apricot puree, fresh from Nonni Trimboli's tree. Even the driest cake disaster would be transformed into the most delicious treat when she was finished. This, however, just felt like the holes were burning larger and larger with her anger. There was nothing sweet to fill up the cavities. How dare he be so arrogant! He presumed to speak for without even checking with her. He dismissed and insulted her family. He ignored and despised what was important to her!

She had wanted to stay engaged for one more night... but as she lay there in the dark, she knew that was pointless. She was not going to marry him. She got up and switched on the lamp by the dressing table. She took off the ring and put it back in its box. She looked at it, glinting in the lamp light, and then snapped the lid closed. The fact that Worsley didn't even understand that she was going to the train station to say goodbye, reinforced to her that perhaps his insight had been limited to just one thing: this was a chasm too wide to traverse.

When the night sky finally started to pale, she got dressed, made a cup of tea and drank it silently. She walked down to the train station with the ring-box in her little handbag. The weight of it felt heavy, weighing her down.

When Worsley saw her step onto the platform, he smiled victoriously. "I knew you would come. I am so glad you saw sense!"

"So am I."

"Have you checked your bags already?"

"Worsley, I have come to return something that is yours." She opened up her handbag and pulled out the ring box.

He stared at her confused. "You are not coming?"

"No. I think the arguments you have made are all very valid. I need to stay here, and you need to go. We cannot be married if we are in two different places." Far apart, more than just geography.

"But Faith, what will I tell everyone? Don't you want to say goodbye?"

"I am here to say goodbye." The train guard blew his whistle, and she stepped back.

"Are you sure? This is unexpected," he said with a frown.

"I am sure... and no, it is not at all unexpected. You were the one who mapped this course. There really is no other way, like you said. This is best. Goodbye Worsley."

The train hissed. And he moved towards the carriage step. "Come back with me Faith. Please. We were perfect together. At home it was different."

She took another step back and shook her head. She mouthed 'Goodbye' as his frame stood in the carriage doorway, his face dawning with the realisation that she really was not going to relent. The train hissed again, steam clouding her vision in a cloud. It slowly chugged out of the station, pouring dark smoke over the platform. She didn't move. In some way it felt fitting, to be shrouded by such dirty, mouth-choking soot. She waited until it cleared, and the train disappeared around the corner. Then she turned on her heel and walked home.

Gabe was sawing timber in his workshop when she walked up the path. He grinned his good morning. "Did you say goodbye to David?"

"I did." Faith swallowed and didn't smile.

Hmm. She really did look shattered that Jones had left. Perhaps he had underestimated her loyalty to David after all. What if she really did love him? He had been hoping she would be relieved he was gone or feel the reprieve of having space to breathe again. He was suffocating her. Gabe watched her run her hand up over her forehead, that nervous gesture so familiar to him. "Oh. You have taken off your ring. Does that mean I get to kiss you now?" he said lightly.

"No, it does not. I... umm... I'm going to do some painting this morning. I didn't want it to get dirty."

"Oh. Alright then." Well, not in a joking mood. "Are you okay?"

"Yes, I'm fine."

"Hmm. I have discovered that a little bit of painting can serve as a great distraction. Good news is that we both need distracting, and that will definitely help meet our timeline."

"Well. Good. On with the plan."

* * *

14.

Faith herded her brothers and sisters up the stairs of the schoolhouse. She introduced them to Miss Rossi, who stood on the verandah, glamourous and painted like a movie celebrity. Violet ogled her crisp dress and tiny waistline. Daisy was reading, jostled by the children milling around to meet the new teacher. No one took very much notice of Mr Kaye at all, as he stood in the background directing traffic.

"Good mornin', Galloway family," said Mirabella.

Jimmy and Joe were hopping on their legs anxious to go and play. "Use your manners please boys," Faith said with a firm hand on their shoulder.

"Good morning, Miss Rossi... Mr Kaye," the boys said with just enough harshness in their tone so they could not be accused outright of mimicking the new teacher. And then they giggled and rushed out to take charge of the game in the yard. Faith prodded Violet who was still staring speechless at Mirabella's outfit, shining in the morning sunlight like the spotlight of stage lights. And then she prompted Daisy standing against the wall with her nose in a book. Eventually the greetings were delivered.

Mirabella smiled innocently as she handed Faith the enrolment sheet to sign. "It seems a certificate wasn't needed to get this job after all," she said in a hoarse whisper.

Faith raised her brow and finished completing the form. She stood up straight, and then said goodbye with a nod. As she was walking along the verandah towards the stairs, she came face to face with the men from the school committee. They were strolling around the school, paternally patting student's heads and nodding to mothers who were fussing over their children, helping them organise their ports on the racks.

"Miss Galloway. Good morning. I would have thought your mother would be dropping off the students this morning... in person."

"Hmm. She is tending to Gus who is running a fever. She sends her apologies."

"Speaking of apologies Miss Galloway, the school committee wishes to formally acknowledge your interest in the teaching position here at the school. However, I think you can see that we are more than happy with the appointment we have made." They looked over to where Mirabella was dazzling parents and children alike.

"Oh yes, I do understand. Miss Rossi is very... beautiful." She didn't have the confidence to use words like competent or capable.

"She will make a fine teacher, and Mr Kaye has much experience," Mr Romano asserted.

"I think it is admirable that the school committee is supporting the post-war gender equality cause so liberally."

Mr Romano cleared his throat. If he was pursuing a cause, it was not equality. "Of course. We are a very progressive school."

Mr Stewart nodded. "Regarding the matter brought to our attention by Mr Jones, we see no reason to adjust our decision. Consequently, you won't need to send any further emissaries on your behalf, Miss Galloway. Our decision is firm."

Faith flushed and nodded. "Noted. I trust your school term goes well. Good day."

She swallowed her humiliation. Of course they would think she sent Worsley to speak to them. She quickly walked down the stairs, across the school yard, nodding blindly to a mother who was hustling her children towards the classrooms. She could still hear Worsley's voice in her head, "*We will see. We will see.*" It did confirm one thing though: she had not lost touch with Lenwick ways while she had been away. It also reinforced that her access to that particular paying job was now officially off the table. Tutoring just became a necessity.

* * *

After school, Faith sat her brothers and sisters down at Nonni Trimboli's kitchen table and plied them with afternoon tea. "How did your first day go?" she asked. The boys ate faster, stuffing their mouths to avoid answering her questions.

Gabe came and pulled up a chair. Faith raised her brow. "I'm taking a break," he said with a shrug. "You're surely not going to make me leave? I don't what to miss out on these tales of adventure."

"Let him stay Faith," was the universal chorus, through full mouths.

"Very well," and she poured him a coffee. "But you have to share with the other children, and use your manners," she said in her very best teacher's voice.

"Yes Miss," Gabe said with a grin. He turned to the kids who continued refilling their mouths with more biscuits. "So," he said in a conspiring whisper, "If Mr Kaye taught the older grades, and Miss Rossi supervised the primary grades... what did you learn?"

Jimmy spoke through the crumbs. "I learnt Miss Rossi has big..."

"James Galloway!" Faith interjected quickly.

"What?" He swallowed the last of his biscuit. "I was just gunna say she has... a big voice. They match each other. Grey-Kaye is a grunter. She is a screecher. I could wind her up like a squeaky old windmill on a windy day. She sounded like her blades would fly off."

"I like her," defended Violet. "She has nice clothes."

Gabe nodded sagely. "But can she read?"

"Not really. She made us do all the reading. I didn't pronounce Argentina properly just to hear her correct me. *Ar-get-atina!*" said Jimmy, squawking like a cockatoo.

"Innovative," commented Gabe as he drank his coffee to smother his smirk.

Faith reached over poured herself a cup of coffee as well.

Joe grinned, determined to match his older brother. "I said I couldn't say Gut-e-malda."

"You really can't pronounce Guatemala," said Daisy with a sigh.

"But she said it worse than me," said Joe with satisfaction.

"Okay, so you did geography. That is ambitious," observed Faith.

"But in the end, we only talked about Italy. Boring." Jimmy was disgusted.

Gabe raised his brow. "Italy can be interesting."

"Nah. We read about Italy; we talked in Italy..."

"Italian," Faith corrected.

"Italy, Italy, Italy."

"No times-tables? No spelling? But you did Reading?"

Daisy looked up from her page. "Of course. I always read," she murmured. She shrugged. "Mr Kaye is exactly the same. He hasn't changed." This unnecessary interrogation was interrupting her story, and she went back to her book.

"Well, we mostly read maps. But Miss Rossi only wanted us to find Italy. Any idiot knows where to find the boot," said Jimmy definitely.

"Not true," sighed Daisy again. "You are always losing your boots."

Faith stood up. "Okay. Well, we will clear up afternoon tea, then I am going to give you some activities to complete. I need to assess what level you are working at. Gabe, would you stay with the others while I do this?" she asked.

"How about they come down to the workshop? I've some things to work on."

"Yes!" said Joe jumping up, scraping back his chair.

Gabe stood up. "Come and have a look at your tutoring room first. Your sister and I have been working on it for you," said Gabe directing them towards the room. The chalk board had been installed. Four coloured desks sat in the room. A wooden planter with tiled inserts on each side, holding a leafy plant, was positioned where the teacher's desk would soon be. There was a cute little note staked in the soil that read: '*Teacher's desk goes here*'.

The kids went quiet as they looked around. This was sending a very strong message that this was a place for serious work. "What's wrong?" Faith asked. "We worked hard on this. I thought you would like it."

Daisy eventually spoke. "This is better than school." She sounded impressed. "I thought we'd just be sitting around the kitchen table."

"Which desk is mine?" asked Jimmy.

"The blue one. Joe has the terracotta. Violet's is the teal-green, and Daisy has the cream one."

"Why can't I have a purple desk?" asked Violet with a frown.

"Purple is not a school colour, Idiot. Where do you sit?" Joe asked Faith.

Faith cleared her throat. "Gabe is still working on a teacher's desk. It's nearly done. And we have some frames to put posters on the wall as well. I thought we would hang maps, but perhaps you have had enough geography for now. Okay. Jimmy you are first; the others can help Gabe. Joe, don't touch anything unless Gabe says you can. I don't want to be paying for broken tools. Gabe you have full license to pull them into line."

"Why can't I go down there," objected Jimmy.

"You can once this is done. The quicker you cooperate, the sooner it will be Joe's turn."

"Wow. I'm really glad you're not our teacher for real, 'cause we would never have any fun."

Faith pulled up a chair beside his desk and plied him with maths, and spelling, and then reading.

"Did I pass?" he asked at the end.

"You don't get a mark. This is so I can assess where you are up. You can go down to the workshop now. Joe's turn." Jimmy ran for the door. "Listen to Gabe!" she reminded him.

Faith went through the assessments for each one. When she finally released Daisy, she sat quietly for a time, and considered the pages before her. It was supposed to be just one year, but she was not convinced that would be enough. Would she stay in Lenwick indefinitely now? Well, she wasn't sure anymore. She had no idea that doing what she believed God wanted of her, would be so challenging. She had sort of imagined that it would be like gliding on top of water. But right now, it felt like wading through mud. Did a person of faith have to give up more than they got back? Was it even worth it? She shook her head. If someone else had said these things to her, she would have been shocked and defended their faith in God's guidance vigorously. But now that she was asking these questions herself, she didn't know. Honestly, right now, very little made sense. But what she did know was that helping her brothers and sisters... this was the right thing to do. They definitely needed help. This much she knew. She could do that part.

* * *

When she returned from dropping the children home, Faith sat by Gabe's bench as he continued to work on her teacher's desk. She looked at the drawers he was installing down the side of her desk, each one decorated with a tiled insert. "Gabe... this is amazing! A simple table would more than suffice."

"A teacher needs a place to put things."

"You are going to a lot of effort when I'm only here for a year."

"Henrik would say that if a job is worth doing, it is worth doing well. A proper desk will be useful down the track."

"It seems that your apprenticeship with the frustrating and pedantic Mr Henrik Wagner gave you an eye for detail. The effort you've put into this is incredible. This is wonderful work."

"I have my own style and way of working. There is no way Old Henrik would allow anyone to hang around in his workshop and distract him while he was working."

"Oh, so now I am distracting you?"

"*Si.* Some things cannot be changed. I like having people about." '*Specifically, I like having you around Faith Galloway,*' he added in his head.

"Well, thanks for helping this afternoon. For our first tutoring session, I think we did okay."

Gabe noticed her use of "our" and "we", and it felt right. But he didn't want to make a big deal of it and shrugged lightly. "I'm guessing Mirabella has only one lesson up her sleeve and tomorrow will not be much different from today."

"She might surprise us all."

"Oh. I will be surprised," he said with a grin.

"I'll fix dinner, so you can you go home."

They ate, and then Gabe sat back. "Will it disturb you if I go back and fiddle in the workshop for a bit? I would like to keep going on this. If I can get a few projects completed, I'll be able to showcase them. It might encourage some orders."

"No problem. I actually find it comforting knowing you are down there working."

"Comforting? When did I go from annoying to comforting?"

"About the same time that I became a distraction, I guess. Don't read too much into that. I just like knowing you are around."

"Huh. Me too. Good night. I'll see you in the morning."

* * *

15.

Faith pushed open the door to the seamstress's little shop and the bell in the doorway tinkled. "Oh Miss Galloway. It is a fine afternoon. Are you getting nervous about the wedding? So many people are getting married. This must be a very exciting time for you."

Faith swallowed. She really did need to seriously think about how she would officially break the news that she was no longer engaged. But if it was known that she was single and unattached, she would probably have to move out of Gabe's house, even if he wasn't staying there officially. She just preferred the way things were. "Oh yes... thank you, Miss Townsend. This is what I came to talk to you about. Since we have pushed the wedding out for a year, I need to put a hold on the gown. Will that be a problem?"

"Well, the fabric you ordered came in, and although I haven't started piecing it, a cancellation fee would be appropriate. It is a very expensive order just to have on hold."

"Oh. Well, yes of course. I am so sorry. I had not expected to delay this."

"Oh no my dear, I didn't mean to suggest anything untoward. There are so many other jobs coming in at the moment, that I am not worried about losing the order like I might have once. I did wonder though; do you think you will apply for the teacher's position once they are married."

"I'm sorry, what?"

"You know. The job at the school, now that Miss Rossi is engaged. You know how the committee is a stickler for the rules."

"Mirabella is engaged... to be married?" This was news. She thought Gabe would be the first to share this news, as it would get him off the hook.

"Oh yes. And her ring... Oh! It is such a beautiful setting. And the design of her wedding dress... oh, she has exquisite taste! She asked me to make it, you know. It is a relief, in a way, to have your order postponed. It takes a lot of time to sew such a gorgeous gown! It is so very fashionable. Just like the magazines."

Faith ignored the implication that her own gown had not measured up to the Rossi standard, even though she had chosen from the book on Miss Townsend's bookshelf. She went fishing for more information. "Oh... and the... groomsmen?"

"Well... there are so many Trimboli brothers and cousins, that Miss Rossi said she expected Gabe would want a large wedding party."

"Gabe?" Faith froze and stared at the money she held in her hand and felt a pain shoot through her chest. "Oh. Of course. Did Mirabella say they had set a date?" She choked and could barely speak.

"Well, Miss Rossi did nominate to collect her gown just after the winter break. And since her dress is not a winter fashion, I'm guessing she has her heart set on a spring wedding. That would be so very flattering."

"I... well, what a lot of sewing you will have to complete in that time. That is not far off really." Less than a year. She pushed the money across the counter. "Can you put this against the cancellation fee, and I'll bring the rest in tomorrow."

"Oh yes, I will be very busy. Are you going to be one of the attendants? You have such a long-standing friendship with the Trimboli family. Warm reds look beautiful on you Faith. I could suggest that to Miss Rossi. Do you remember that first little dress I made for you as a child? I can still see you choosing your ribbon. Such a beautiful shade. That was quite an occasion."

"Miss Townsend, I am sorry, again, to put my order on hold." Faith turned and quickly walked outside. It was hard for her to stay focused. Gabe had finally conceded. Why hadn't he said something? Why did she always assume that life, in some way, could stabilise and stay the same? But it never did.

* * *

She walked straight into the spare room where Gabe was working on some casement windows positioned across some trestles. "Hi. You're back earlier than expected. How's your mother?" He looked at her face and put down the putty knife in his hand. "Is everything okay?"

"Congratulations," she said simply.

"Thank you. What for?"

"Your engagement."

"Is this a proposal? Because I thought that was the groom's responsibility. Even though I know you prefer a modern approach, I would still expect you to be un-engaged first."

"Very funny. Miss Townsend just told me she has been commissioned to make Mirabella's wedding gown... since *you...* are now *engaged.*"

"Who me? Engaged. To Mirabella?" He rubbed the back of his neck. "Wouldn't I know about this?"

She went to say something smart, and then stopped as she looked at his face. "You really didn't know? Gabe, would she truly announce this to force your hand?"

He picked up a rag and wiped his hands. "You know, I need to go out for a bit. This definitely deserves a conversation."

She put out her arm as he went to walk past her. He stopped and looked at her with a raised brow. "Gabe? Gabe... um... Perhaps I should tell you that Worsley gave me an ultimatum before he left. He said I was to go back with him, or he would break our engagement. Obviously, I didn't leave. Umm... all that to say... that I am, in fact... un-engaged now... as you said." She held up her left hand. "Not just protecting it from paint splatters... sorry I didn't tell you."

"Huh? How about that?" He paused, still wiping his hands on the rag. An urge to sweep her into his arms and to kiss her full on the mouth flushed over his body. Instead, he continued to wipe his hands. "Well, that is certainly the most sensible thing I have heard in a while. He wasn't the right David for you. I still stand by that." He titled his head. "Why didn't you tell me?"

"Because... I thought you would not let me stay. You were very clear that being engaged was one of the criteria that made it appropriate for me to rent your rooms. I didn't want to jeopardise my tenancy."

"So, I'm good for a house?"

"Not exactly...well, you know what I mean..." Her voice trailed off. It sounded cheap and demeaning.

"Actually... I'm not sure I do get the full meaning of this. Look, can we talk about this later? I have an engagement to get out of. School will be out soon, and I need to catch Mirabella before much more is set in motion. Perhaps it is all a big misunderstanding, and she has actually given up, and is engaged to someone else. You never know my luck. There have been a few bees hanging around her honeypot. Levi Martin has seemed particularly enthusiastic."

He put down the rag and went to go, but then paused and turned around. "Faith, will you marry me?"

"I'm sorry, what?"

"If I can tell Mirabella I have already asked you... and you said 'yes', that will make my case that I can't be engaged to her far less complicated."

"To dodge Mirabella's clutches?"

"You did say that if I needed anything, that I only needed to ask."

"Wow. You really do know how to fill out a blank cheque. I wasn't thinking of an engagement when I offered that. I'll say yes, and we can talk about it later. Just go and sort it out. Miss Townsend is going to be heartbroken when she finds out she can't make that dress."

"I'll be heartbroken if she does."

* * *

"Good afternoon, Mirabella. I hear you are engaged," said Gabe standing up from where he was sitting on the steps of the teacher's cottage, as Mirabella opened the squeaking gate and walked up the path.

She looked around and opened the door. "Come inside Gabriele. It is not fitting to stand on the verandah like this."

"I'm not coming inside. What I came to say, can be said out here." She came over and draped her arms around his neck. He firmly removed them and stepped back. "I am not engaged to you."

"Of course. I know that. But it is going to happen eventually. I am just getting ready for when it does," she said.

"I wish you had spoken with me before you made these very public arrangements... because now this is quite embarrassing. You should know, I am already engaged to someone else. I have asked another lady, and she said yes. I cannot be engaged to you at the same time."

"But I got in first! I did. You were engaged to me first."

"Mirabella, that does not even make sense. Whenever you have talked about this, I have been very specific. I am not going to marry you. Why do you insist on pretending it is otherwise?"

"No! That is a lie! Your mother said that we would be married! We are destined to be together. Our parents have arranged this. She said it is something they have organised since we were children. You have to do what they say! It is proper and right! You cannot disobey."

"Mamma? You think Mamma put you up to this? Now I think that is even more delusional than just ignoring what is really going on. I am not engaged to you, and I am not going to marry you. This has not changed."

Mirabella's eyes looked panicked. "No! It is true. She said that! You have to agree. I've used my wages to put a deposit on the gown, and a ring."

"Which is not a ring I bought for you. Where you spend your money is your prerogative Mirabella. I am not responsible for your purchases."

"You are, if it is for our wedding."

"It is not our wedding because we are not engaged."

"We are! We are!" she screeched.

Gabe shook his head bewildered. How could she not hear what he was saying? "Flattering no less Mirabella. Look, you are a beautiful woman. There are plenty of men around here who would be thrilled to be your groom. I don't understand why you insist that it has to be me. You have a job. You are an independent, modern woman. Find a man who wants to make you happy. You can do that."

"But your mother really did say…"

"Hmm. Think about it, Mirabella. Your heart knows what I say is true. Of all the people who have paid attention to you, and sent you flowers, since you have arrived in Lenwick... which one do *you* want to marry. You decide. You have a ring and a dress. That makes it easy for him. Find that person."

"But I want that person to be you. I want to marry you. I will make a good wife."

"Like I said, I am already engaged to someone else."

"But you never said anything about that before. And your mother said..."

"I never said anything because we were keeping it private... like a romantic secret. A secret that is now out of the bag, by the way, because you circulated the notion that *we* are engaged, when we are actually not. Just talk to the next guy before you order the cake. That would be best." He turned on his heel and left, leaving Mirabella stammering and staring after him.

He went down to the river and sat there for a bit... just looking at the shimmer of afternoon sunlight on the water. He prayed for calm, like the lazy water drifting along before him. Calm before the storm of his mother's disapproval.

"Mamma?"

"Gabriele! Good afternoon figlio mio!"

"Mamma... I have something to tell you."

"Si? Just in time. I have baked some fresh biscotti. Almond ones. Your favourite."

"Thanks. Mamma, I have come to tell you that I am engaged," he said as he poured coffee from the pot on the stove.

"Oh, my beautiful figlio! This is magnificent news! Wonderful! You make such a handsome couple. Such beautiful grand-babies you will have!"

"Yes, I hope so. Although, you should know, that I am engaged to Faith. Faith Galloway... not Mirabella."

"What? No! That Galloway girl is already engaged to someone else. She told me she was promised to that other man... that city fellow... the tall one. Do not tell me you are a home-breaker Gabriele Trimboli! This is bad. Very bad. I will not have it!"

"Her engagement was broken off; between them – not by me. Now she is engaged to me." For now... but for how long he was not sure. What a mess.

"No, you cannot! She is not even Italian! I knew it was a bad idea that she stay at Nonni's house! This is bad!"

"Mamma..."

"You have to marry Mirabella. Her parents and your Papa, we talk. She is so beautiful. You could love her. Many of the boys already do."

"I am not going to marry Mirabella. I am marrying Faith."

"Oh, come figlio mio. Gabriele, you surely have got over her by now. It was just a childhood crush. You have to grow up!"

"Mamma, we are in Australia now. You do not get to organise my wife for me. I have always wanted to marry Faith. You know that." He picked up the biscotti and nodded. "Your almond biscotti is still the best Mamma," he said as he walked out.

* * *

Gabe strapped on his tool belt. His father strolled over and stood there. He said nothing.

"Papa?"

His father cleared his throat. "There is not much that I fight your Mamma on. I learnt that early on. But this business... with Mirabella... it is wrong that you refuse. Why can't you just go along with it? She will make you a pretty wife."

"Papa. Mamma is not asking me to change the design of a cabinet I am making. She wants me to marry someone I don't even respect. I have to live with this for the rest of my life. I have asked Faith. She said yes."

"Si? Why can't you be like your brothers and your cousins? They all have nice Italian girls."

"Well, perhaps that is good for them. Faith is good for me."

"Bah! I thought that when she went away that you would... you know... move on. She is bad for you Gabriele. She is not someone for our family. I even had Nonni talk to her... to encourage her to go... to get her away from Lenwick... away from you."

"Nonni would never do that! She knew how I felt. She knew I would not give up on her. And I haven't." But even as he said this, he heard Faith's voice echoing in his head saying Nonni was her greatest advocate. Nonni had encouraged her to leave. Nonni had been just another person pushing them apart. The betrayal of that thought cut deeply.

"Si. You marry Mirabella. It is the right thing to listen to your Mamma and Papa. It is right to obey your parents. The Good Book says it, 'obey your Mamma and Papa. Even you know this is true."

"Papa, I am not fourteen anymore. This is not some rebellious teenage crush to defy you and Mamma. I am a grown man, and I can make my own choices about who I spend the rest of my life with. That is right too. You know that I love you. This is not a matter of honour, or obedience, or disobedience."

But even as he said it... he wondered. What if God was calling him in on the verandah and telling him to marry Mirabella. What if that was what was happening here? Was this something that he had to do, even when he didn't want to?

* * *

Gabe put down his fork. "So, what is it like being engaged to me? Italian name, and all. I could see you as Mrs Trimboli. Mrs Faith Trimboli sounds right to me. You know I will have to give you a ring, so that Mirabella can see I was completely serious... about not being available."

"It's kind of funny, don't you think? That after all these years we are finally engaged. I'm a little shocked you told your parents though. Why would you put yourself through that?"

"Why not? They all have to believe it."

"Because you were not serious. You just needed an escape from Mirabella. I mean, it's not real... is it?"

"Well, I did ask you. In fact, you are the only woman I have ever proposed to. I believe this is round three. I don't make a habit of just randomly selecting a wife. This has been a long time in the coming." He paused then and looked at her softly. "I *really* want it to be real. Marry me for real Faith."

She stared at him for a moment, and pushed back from the table, standing up. "Umm... Oh. For real? I wasn't expecting this. I know we have been in various states of entanglement since I was nine. But I thought... I thought it was finished."

"Faith, I have never thought this was finished. Not once."

"Really? Never?"

"Well, okay. Once. And I have regretted what I said then ever since. But I do put that outburst down to a very unfortunate case of adolescent egotism and pigheadedness. I simply plead insanity, Your Honour."

She smiled and shook her head. "I'm not sure insanity is helping your case, Mr Gabriele Trimboli."

"Then there is more evidence that I wish to submit." He paused and stood up; coming over to her, he offered her his hand. "Faith... can I show you something?"

"Okay... Sure."

He escorted her into the tutoring classroom. He went over to the potted plant, with the note staked in the soil: '*Teacher's desk goes here*'. He knelt down and lifted the planter aside. There on the polished timber floor was the undeniable shape of a heart in rustic red paint, creased as if it had been pressed with fabric, marked with scratches across its surface. "You knocked the paint tin when you were painting the sills. There wasn't much paint left in the tin and I didn't think it would soak through the drop-sheet, but it did. It did... and it formed this heart. I couldn't stop looking at it when I pulled up the sheets. It felt like us. Faith, you asked why we didn't have the same story as a lot of others around here. But what if we have our own story? Sure, what we have is unpredictable and it may even seem accidental... but it works. We work. We do. Just like this heart. And I know it is not shaped perfectly, and I know it has scratches on the surface, but I want us to be more than childhood friends, more than landlord and tenant. I want us to be partners, life partners... husband and wife." He pulled a worn ring case from his pocket and presented it to her, still kneeling over the heart. "Marry me, Faith. Please, will you marry me for real?"

She stared at the ring. Three rubies set side by side: worn and familiar; fine scratches across the surface. She shook her head affectionately. "This is Nonni's ring. You are really serious about this."

"It is. I am."

"Ahh... rubies for your Ruby Girl. Gabe, this is very unfair... because if I say no, that will mean two broken engagements in the space of a very short time."

"So... just say 'yes'."

"When I heard Mirabella had a ring and ordered her dress, and was telling everyone she was engaged to you, it terrified me no end. I just exploded inside. I was so confused and yet I told myself I had no right to be jealous or hurt, because I wasn't yours... and you were not mine. I was shocked by that because I never felt like that with Worsley. I was sad and angry with him for sure... but not surprised when he left ... not really. This was completely different."

"Hmm... is that a 'yes' then?"

"But it did make me realise one thing. I think... in my head, and in my heart... I believed you were already mine. You have always been mine. I never realised that before. Or admitted it."

"So, it is a 'yes'?"

"I kept hearing Nonni's voice in my head. '*Do not give up. Promise me you will not settle.*' I always thought she was talking about going away... but now it feels like she was actually saying I was not to give up and settle for other's people's expectations if *this* is what I want. Gabe, I think she was telling me not to give up on you."

"Then... please, listen to Nonni... make your answer a 'yes'."

"Yes."

He raised his eyebrows. "Yes?"

She nodded. "It is a yes. Yes. Nonni was right. She was always right. This is right. Yes."

A grin spread over his face, as he slid the ring over her finger.

Her hand closed in around it, holding it tight. "It is so perfect that we have Nonni's ring. I have always loved it."

"Your ring now. Faith Galloway... you have made me a very happy man." He stood up and gently pulled her toward him. "I said I'd kiss you when you took off your ring. I didn't expect that it would be to put a ring on your finger."

"But..."

He smothered her objection with a kiss. He paused for a moment. "I am forever grateful Nonni. So very grateful," and he kissed her again. He pulled away and seriously looked into her eyes. "You do know this scratched little heart has stamped its own seal on Nonni's house and it means I can't possibly sell it now. Welcome home Faith! We are home."

* * *

16.

"Faith... would you come with me? I want to show you something."

She frowned as he gathered his keys. "Now? It's lunch time. I only have a couple of hours before school gets out."

Gabe grabbed her hand and pulled her out to his ute that was parked on the street. He turned the key, and it lurched forward and stalled. He cleared his throat as he started it again. "Faith, I'm sorry we never went on any dates."

"Oh, I don't know. We've had a dinner together every evening since I arrived back. Surely that counts..."

"Well, I wanted to take you on a proper date... a picnic. Just the two of us. For lunch."

She grinned and shook her head. "You do know there really is no need to court me. I have already said yes."

"Yeah, I know, but I feel that we missed something, doing it back to front like this. Still, I guess we were never ones to stick to the usual script." He pulled up outside an industrial looking shed that had been used as warehouse. The building was set on a large block. Bits of old junk and broken pallets were lying around. Gabe offered his hand to Faith as he opened the passenger door, then he lifted out a basket and a rug from the back of the ute. They walked over to the shed through the straggly grass, around a few tiger-pear cactus plants that were scattered in their path.

She looked around and shook her head. "I am going to suggest that it is a good thing I have already said yes to your proposal before you tried dating me. If this is your idea of a romantic outing, we really do need to work on your sense of romance."

He grinned. "Perhaps it doesn't matter where... just as long as we are together."

"Hmm," she said shaking her head with a smile. "It still needs work."

He pulled open the door to the warehouse and ushered her inside. It was a fairly large building, spacious inside. There were cobwebs and old stuff cluttering the space. The timbered floor was dusty, and the walls and ceiling consisted of exposed beams. "Hmm. I feel like we are sneaking out of school again and hiding out in that old shed by the creek. As I remember, we got caught and Mrs James was very severe in her punishment. It took the edge off that little adventure."

"See... a romantic adventure. I kissed you in that abandoned shack." He kissed her lightly to reinforce his point.

She looked around. "What did they use this place for?"

"It was connected to the sawmill at one point, and then it was used as a goods dispersal outlet for the railway. Do you remember your father ever talking about it?"

"Not really..."

"Hmm..." Gabe flicked out the rug in the middle of the floor, and they spluttered at the dust that puffed up. Together they arranged their picnic, sitting in the muted shadows, watching the play of sunlight streaming through the high grimy windows lighting up streaks of disturbed dust particles floating in the air.

As they ate, Faith chatted about some of the things she had been organising for their wedding day. "I've had another fitting with Miss Townsend. She is pleased that she has the go ahead to start my dress again.

When I showed the girls my design, Violet instantly had some suggestions to change the bodice. She insists that it needs to be different from the original pattern, which I agree. Violet says she got her ideas from some of Mirabella's outfits. When I showed Mrs Townsend her suggestions, she was excited to make the alterations. And she did take the on-hold fee off the price, which I am very grateful for. I am, after all, just a humble tutor." She spoke about her bouquet, which would be a half dozen simple white lilies in keeping with her middle name. Overall, she was satisfied their planning was progressing well enough.

When they finished lunch, Gabe looked around the warehouse with a sweeping gesture. "So... when I went looking for properties, I found this place. I investigated to see if I could buy it, and it so happens that it is for sale, and quite reasonably priced. It is near the railway line... which is a problem if you want to sleep-in because the train passes by early in the morning... but during the day it is quiet here. I think the property has great potential."

"Ahh. Now I understand. You want to make this your next renovator. But the point of a renovation is to sell it on afterwards. You've already said the area is not suitable as residential. I cannot see anyone willing to pay money for a beautifully renovated storehouse. Especially now they have moved the railway station to the other side of town. Think about this carefully Gabe, or you may find you have capitalised on a property no one will want."

"You are right. It's lack of utility means there is virtually no competition... and that actually adds to the appeal. No offers have ever been made on it. None, and I'm sure I could get the owner to drop the price even more," he said with confidence. He reached inside his vest jacket and pulled out a couple of folded pieces of paper. "I drew up some concept sketches.

Faith I really need your thoughts on this before I proceed." He handed them over tentatively.

She frowned and unfolded the papers slowly, wondering. She stared at each one for a long time. Gabe held his breath, as she looked around and then back to the first sheet, rotating it slowly.

"Do you see what I see?" he asked softly.

"It's quiet, you say...during the day?"

"Not a peep. That's not likely to change unless they start running trains more than twice a week. But even if they did, I don't think it would be too disruptive. Not really."

Faith ran her hand up over her forehead. "Umm... I don't know what to say..."

"Say yes. We can do this Faith. We can. You are tutoring more students than that little room at home can hold. You are turning parents away every week. More and more, they are looking for an alternative to the public school. Kids are dropping out because it is wasting their time being there. This gives the district another option."

"You want to transform this shed... into a schoolhouse."

"It is the perfect setting as a hub of learning and stimulating young minds. The area is big enough, with enough room to partition off some office and storage space. Lenwick could have its own little private school. You will be its principal teacher. I could help with the setup, grounds and administration. We can do this."

"Why now, so close to our wedding?"

"Well, a couple of reasons. One is that I'm partial to the idea of having our home back just for us, particularly as we start our life together as husband and wife."

"It is going to take a bit to get it ready."

"Sure. We only have to start with a basic clean-up. The structure is solid, so most of what it needs is cosmetic, lining the walls and ceiling, which can be done progressively. A Trimboli family working bee would get a good jump on the necessities. We can put a high fence and hedge along the railway boundary. A few gardens will increase the aesthetic appeal dramatically. The block is large, so there's room for a playground. You might as well teach your sisters and brothers during school time, so they can get their afternoons back. You can keep the after-school tutoring hours if you need to. This gives you more space for that."

"Well, we do have desks... and the colours we have chosen, could be allocated according to each scholastic level. Terracotta for the little ones; blue for grades four to six... and so on."

"And as we take enrolments, they do so on the understanding that the premises are a work in progress."

"If we start this now, I will need to teach after we are married."

"Of course. Can't start a school and then not have a teacher for it. Mrs James taught right up until she was pregnant. Being married didn't stop her from being an excellent teacher. You've said so yourself."

"If we can't find another suitable teacher, it might mean I need to continue teaching, even after we have children." She said it to test him. He expected him to be scandalised, to quickly back track and rethink the whole thing. Faith's frown deepened. She slowly took a drink and stared at the paper in her hand. She had this same conversation with Worsley... only this time she was the one playing devil's advocate. Did she really want to work when she had a family? How could she start something so bold, and then just abandon it? Did it really have to be either/or, as everyone said?

Gabe smiled. They had never really talked about children, but it was always part of the dream. He was pleased having their own family was not off the table. "I come from a long line of strong working women, who never let a ring... or children, stop them from investing hard. You never know... your mother's particular liking for babies might mean she may help with her grandchildren. Besides, this endeavour would be like our very first brainchild that we have together. It would not be at all like you to abandon it."

Faith looked up at him. He had just responded to the echoes in her head, reassuring her. The loudest argument of his case was 'together'... not just a project. Not just a job. Not just work. Life.

"Well? Is that a 'yes'? Do you need time?"

"I think it is... yes. Yes. It is a 'yes'."

"Really?" A grin spread over his face. "We are doing this?"

"It is pretty good. How long have you been working on this?"

"A while..." Gabe lifted his glass, tilting it in a toast. "Well congratulations Miss Galloway... you have just secured yourself a teaching job, a schoolhouse, a builder and renovator, an administrator and a groundsman, all in one afternoon. We'll see your mother when we take the kids home this afternoon and make an offer. I've already spoken to her; I told her we just needed to firm the details. You being the most important detail of course."

"I'm sorry? What has Ma'ma got to do with this? I think locking in babysitting services at this stage might be a tad premature."

"I might be advocating for that large Italian family expectation after all. Didn't you say fifteen kids was the goal? We have catch up to do."

"Gabe..."

He laughed at her. "This shed was bought by your father, when he went into partnership at the mill. But with the depression, and the war... and then they moved the train station as well, it was never really used as he thought it might be. Your mother owns this."

"I don't understand. Dad owned this? With the mill? But they bought out his part of the business when he died."

"Yes, however this property was never included in the sale. Your mother thought it was, but it was missed somehow. She followed it up and she actually holds the separate title. All the rates were paid automatically from your father's trust. I offered to buy it from her, but she is resisting me. I think she is more inclined to set it up independently as a tribute to your father. She was talking about calling the school the "Flynn Galloway Academy". Either way... this is your new classroom."

"Gabe, I need to retract a statement I made earlier. I said you had no idea about first dates... but this... I'm lost for words. You are actually very good at dating. This exceeds any romantic notion I could have conjured up."

* * *

17.

That picnic in the shed catapulted them into a flurry of planning, and cleaning and working. Gabe's initiative was interpreted as a mutiny by some, and successful problem solving by others. It effectively divided the community into two camps... the established schoolhouse group and the independent school faction. Mr Romano mobilised a move against the new school by challenging zoning approvals. Mirabella shone, glittering and glorious in the limelight. Mr Kaye retracted into the background, annoyed that education had become a political football.

Then there was the family discussion that the issue generated. Gabe's father, always the diplomat, quietly refused to take sides. His mother, not so much. The controversy of the school, in his mother's eyes, was another version of the same scandal created when Gabe chose Faith over the beautiful Mirabella. She was heartbroken when Gabe refused to collaborate with her own plans for a large Italian wedding. Levi Martin was seen with Mirabella a lot, even during school hours, doing her bidding, mesmerised by her glorious smile. Then suddenly, quite unexpectedly, Mirabella announced her engagement to Mr Antonio Romano... of the school committee fame. Gabe's mother mourned that it was not her son who was going to get all the lovely press from this wedding, and suffered through her disappointment, less than silently. With the heartbreak of ballads, Levi retreated into hiding.

There was another undeniable factor that fed into this school controversy for Gabe's family. Miss Rossi became bolder in her unconventional lessons that revolved around Italian culture. Increasingly, it was reported that the younger Trimboli nephews were acting up at school and getting into trouble. When Miss Rossi found her students' behaviour out of control, she would take the restless children down to the creek to go fishing. More than one student slipped and fell in the water. Not surprisingly any subject that was boring became an exercise in how quickly they could escalate the situation so they would be released outside. Mirabella would sit on a rock, fanning her face with a magazine under the shade of a tree, in preference to spending time with spelling words inside. Some parents exerted pressure to call Miss Rossi in for an explanation. She unapologetically declared academia was Mr Kaye's area of expertise, and the extra-curricular activities, explored by the committee during her interview, were fitting for active country students. Mr Romano and the school committee were adequately satisfied with the report that she gave. Her relaxed teaching was given the tick of approval, and the three R's remained seriously neglected in her classes.

Mayor Saxton chaired the community meetings regarding the school zoning approval, quickly spiralled into comparing curriculum. Gabe defended their proposal by pointing out curriculum had no relevance to zoning permits, and the topic had become a decoy diverting attention from the real issue, which was that they were being unreasonably stone-walled in their legitimate application. Mirabella stood up and confidently offered her opinion like a squawking parrot. "Children's learning is more bigger than reading and writing." Mr Kaye blushed, Faith rolled her eyes and Gabe again returned to the point at hand: the permit.

The town council battled to adjudicate the issue of zoning permits and there was a great deal of discussion around how realistic it was for a little community to support two schools. Wherever Faith went, she was bombarded with questions, opinions and accusations about splitting a peaceful community unnecessarily.

Even the kids jumped on board this debate. Faith sat with them as they aired their views. Jimmy believed fishing needed to remain a school subject. "No doubt you do Jimmy... but this is an excellent example of being distracted from the main point of the discussion. Fishing does not support the main issue of your education."

"But I can already read and write, just like Daisy said."

"And you can already fish... so again, this is not a logical argument to support your case. You can do better James Galloway. Don't get sloppy in your thinking."

"It is stupid that we can't just do what everyone else does. Their parent's let them."

"We are not beholden to follow other people's choices... particularly poor ones. Ma'ma considers this is a better option for you."

"Huh. This is your stupid idea. And Gabe's. Mum doesn't care too much about school."

"That is where you are wrong. Ma'ma cares very much about your education. She cares so much she is funding the new schoolhouse."

"I ain't going to any stupid school in a stupid old shed," he said defiantly.

"Well. Perhaps. But if you stay at the other school, that means you will have to continue tutoring after school like we have been doing, while your brother and sisters go fishing without you when school is over." Faith smiled sympathetically at the look of disgust that filled his face. At least, on this point, she suspected his resistance would fade.

Every time Faith heard Mirabella's "more bigger" quote repeated like a mantra around the streets and loungerooms of Lenwick, she wondered how this hadn't sealed her fate. Yet in some way, the accidental speech, coupled with the sympathetic idea that English was not her first language, it became a slogan that appealed to the unpretentious, practical, hands-on nature of the community. "Gabe, it is outrageous! They are not just advocating that rudimentary education be neglected! It has been openly sabotaged. Then they justify it, by calling her ignorant laziness 'well-rounded'. It is a terrible rationale for not investing in serious scholarship. Even Jimmy has superior thought-out arguments. These are no longer just unconventional ideas, now it is blatant incompetence! Did you have any idea this school project would become so controversial? Is this what you signed up for?"

"I signed on, not because I thought it would be easy... but because it supports what the kids need. Not everyone will be on board... I know it. But you are a gifted teacher, and if the school committee won't give you an opportunity to do what you are called to do, then I figured that there has to be another way. Just because it is hard, doesn't make it less right."

"I don't know... it just feels like I'm trying to force something that wasn't meant to be. I seriously thought the committee would eventually come around when they saw Miss Rossi in action. But that didn't happen. Mirabella will be married to Mr Romano soon, so by their own assertion there will possibly be a vacancy soon. Perhaps I was just meant to hold on and wait it out."

"Or perhaps they will just revert to giving Mr Kaye back his classes. There will be no need for the second teacher now the enrolments have fallen off. I'm definitely not on board with the idea of you teaching at that

babysitting service if it delays our wedding in any way. Tell me, on the train...
was it about holding a job at the public school, or teaching kids?"

"I can hardly remember. 'Teach the children', I think. I guess I
assumed it was about the school because that was the only Lenwick option I
knew of. It has to be about teaching. That is why I started the tutoring."

"See. Just because it doesn't line up neatly and is a bit scratched... just
because we have to work out how we do it and what it looks like, that doesn't
mean we are not on the right track. Your faith is not misplaced here."

"Gabe... aren't you disappointed that you didn't get called onto the
verandah as well?"

"You're assuming I didn't."

"Were you?"

"Well... I will confess, I was panicked there for a bit. I had this
thought: what if Mirabella was my verandah moment? What if it wasn't just
Mamma's misplaced ideas of tradition, or Papa's desire to keep things smooth,
but God actually wanted me to do that? Would I do it? I don't know. It
messed me around for a while. But then I remembered the backyard. A
backyard is only a yard because it has a fence. God would not ask me to do
something outside his moral boundaries. Basic principles of kindness, respect
and honesty... those fence lines are not fluid. One of my big problems with
Mirabella is that these are things that she bends and blurs, without remorse...
at the drop of a hat, whenever it suits her. I'm to seek those values of the
Kingdom of God first... then the other stuff will be added. That means I have
permission to play in the cubbyhouse with you, if that is what I want to do,
because Mirabella is jumping the fence. This is what I want Faith. I want to
do this with you. That is the desire of my heart."

"You are a remarkable man, Gabe Trimboli. You might even be a David," she said with a grin.

"As long as I am *your* David, I don't mind whether I am remarkable or not. Besides, just hanging around remarkable people like your good self, lifts the standard of normal. We can do this. Controversy, or otherwise. We will find a way to teach the children of Lenwick... help them realise their potential. This is what you have been called to... what *we* have been called to."

* * *

Gabe organised a family working-bee to clean up the warehouse block. This also aired some divided loyalties. But there were still a few Trimboli cousins who held to the axiom that 'blood is thicker than water'. They rolled up willing to help with farm trucks, wheelbarrows, kids, buckets, brooms, mowers and rakes. Faith's mother came with the children and placed Violet on Edith-Rose duty while the others pulled on their gloves and joined in tackling the clean-up. The junk around the building was removed. The grass was slashed back and raked. The inside of the building was emptied, and salvageable items distributed to interested parties. A water cart arrived, and the brooms came out to scrub the building top to bottom, inside and out. Gabe hung a wooden sign over the entry, carved and painted: 'Flynn Galloway Academy'.

A couple of long trestle tables were set up under a tree and lunch was served. Some old packing pallets were broken up to fuel a fire so they could boil a billy or two. Gabe stood up at the table and raised his mug in a toast. "Thank you all for coming and pitching in. Let's make a toast: to all the students who will learn here. May God bless the endeavours of the *Flynn Galloway Academy*." There was a murmur of affirmations from around the table. "And to my lovely Faith, who has the heart and hard work to see this vision materialise." Faith reached over and squeezed Gabe's hand as he sat down. He looked into her eyes and smiled. "One of Lenwick's greatest treasures is finally mine... worth more than rubies. Welcome to my big, busy, beautiful family Faith," he said. "With all of its scratches."

Faith looked around at those gathered at the trestle table, as they helped themselves to cheese laden flatbread and pasta dishes. This is what she missed in the city: the feel of home and family; industry, and community... even in the face of strained loyalties, and polarised perspectives. Faith titled her head as Gabe helped himself to some risotto. "Would it be terrible if we name our first child David?" she asked. "You said the notion was an Italian one, even if the name is not."

He laughed. "No doubt our daughter may have some questions about that! But she would carry any name with dignity, I am sure. Just like her mother. Faith is the perfect name for my wife. David is a fitting name for our child."

Faith smiled to herself. "*Scratches*," Gabe had said. Scratches like on the surface of Nonni's perfect little cameo, and the ring that she now wore on her finger. Beauty, with all of the imperfections imposed by life. This is what makes our faith courageous and strong. She lent in and whispered with a kiss. "Thank you, Gabe Trimboli. Thank you for joining me in this little backyard adventure. I think this is our way of stepping out of the sandpit and starting to climb that imposing tree. What an incredible venture we are on together!"

* * *

The end

Other books by this author

Matt's Boys of Wattle Creek

Maggie & Minotaur

Rose's Diary

Gems of Australia Series:
Sapphires of Hope
Rubies of Ambition
Emerald Dreams

Homes of Healing Series:
The Beachside Cottage
Petra Downs
The Writer's Retreat

Guthrie's Lot Series:
A Spacious Place
A Level Path
The Crying Tree

Pioneers of Grace Series:

Time of Grace

Circle of Grace

Journey of Grace

Mask of Grace

Crucible of Grace

Sculpture of Grace

Bottlebrush Grove Series

Shadows in the Corners

The Ragged Edges

Scratches across the Surface

Cracked through the Core

Children's Book

The Bush Olympics.